PurgeAtory

You Can Purge Your Karma

Brieanne K. Tanner

With Artwork by
Rebecca Goldthorpe and Janessa Rohweller

BALBOA
PRESS
A DIVISION OF HAY HOUSE

Copyright © 2016 Brieanne K. Tanner.

All rights reserved. No part of this book may be used or reproduced by any means, graphic, electronic, or mechanical, including photocopying, recording, taping or by any information storage retrieval system without the written permission of the author except in the case of brief quotations embodied in critical articles and reviews.

Balboa Press books may be ordered through booksellers or by contacting:

Balboa Press
A Division of Hay House
1663 Liberty Drive
Bloomington, IN 47403
www.balboapress.com
1 (877) 407-4847

Because of the dynamic nature of the Internet, any web addresses or links contained in this book may have changed since publication and may no longer be valid. The views expressed in this work are solely those of the author and do not necessarily reflect the views of the publisher, and the publisher hereby disclaims any responsibility for them.

The author of this book does not dispense medical advice or prescribe the use of any technique as a form of treatment for physical, emotional, or medical problems without the advice of a physician, either directly or indirectly. The intent of the author is only to offer information of a general nature to help you in your quest for emotional and spiritual well-being. In the event you use any of the information in this book for yourself, which is your constitutional right, the author and the publisher assume no responsibility for your actions.

Any people depicted in stock imagery provided by Thinkstock are models, and such images are being used for illustrative purposes only. Certain stock imagery © Thinkstock.

Print information available on the last page.

ISBN: 978-1-5043-6379-2 (sc)
ISBN: 978-1-5043-6380-8 (e)

Balboa Press rev. date: 08/12/2016

Dedication

This book is dedicated to my best friend in my youth who passed away abruptly in 1999, Hernan Rodrigo Vasquez, and to my beloved husband, Brian Scott Tanner, my adorable and lovable son, Evan James Tanner. It is also dedicated to all those that haven't found their voices yet, and to those that are scared to speak up. It is my hope and aspiration that this book will inspire those suffering to heal their lives and to understand there is a way to reverse your karmic mental patterns through various healing modalities, and finally to understand there really is a way out.

Epigraph

"It's a little more like the image of a caterpillar, enclosing itself in a cocoon in order to go through a metamorphosis. To emerge as a butterfly, the caterpillar doesn't say, "Well Now. I'm going to climb into this cocoon and come out a butterfly. It's just an inevitable process. It's inevitable. It's just happening. It's got to happen that way. We're talking about a metamorphosis. We're talking about going from a caterpillar to butterfly. We're talking about how to become a butterfly. I mean, the caterpillar isn't walking around saying: Man I'll soon be a butterfly because as long as he's busy being a caterpillar, he can't be a butterfly. It's only when caterpillarness is done that one starts to be a butterfly. And that again is part of this paradox. You cannot rip away caterpilarness. The whole trip occurs in an unfolding process under which you have no control. Well: what am I doing here if I have no control? That's a hard one! Can't I say this is nonsense? You mean I don't have a choice? You're lecture changed my whole life! You think that's choice? Can't I say this is important? No. Not at all. It's an unfolding process." *-Ram Dass from the book, Be Here Now*

Foreword

Sometimes in life, our insignificant moments cross paths with others, and at the intersection, we are blessed by an experience; an opportunity or a person who changes our life permanently - that's exactly what happened between Brieanne and I.

A moment of curiosity on my part, led me to explore *KU, a creative social network application*, a couple of years ago. As someone quite unaccustomed to using social networks or sharing my creative writing, I didn't know what to expect; but I imagined it to be a "flash in the pan" type of scenario. I certainly wasn't prepared for the tremendous journey which it took me on!

Brieanne, also known by the handle's Brieanne and Brie_Kali on the writing apps, was one of the first people I met on KU. We instantly connected on a deep visceral level, and I would describe her as a "soul friend." I liked her quiet, gentle spirit, but it was her gift for weaving magic with words; which really drew me to her. I quickly became an avid reader of her haiku, and our friendship has grown incredibly close since then.

Our friendship stemmed from an online writing application and we also live 5906.68 km / 3670.24 miles apart, but as the saying goes "Closeness has nothing to do with distance" and we know each other inside out. Since those first few months on KU, life has evolved and so has our friendship. We have both become committed writers on the writer's application, *Lettrs* and Brieanne is a regular entrant to my weekly writing prompt entitled, the "Skylark Challenge."

Brie's writing has a strong spiritual quality and is often based on her attraction to the Eastern Arts. She refers to her yoga experiences in particular. Yoga is a fundamental part of Brie's day, much like it is for Liv, the main character in Purge-A-Tory. Her practice begins before dawn because it's a time of peace and stillness.

Healing arts are another commonality between us; although I prefer Tai Chi. Brie and I are similarly programmed, in that, neither of us can imagine not having this space to be in touch with spirit and nature. The oneness of breathing in rhythm - expanding lungs in unison to the sound of birds in the early morning is a powerful and energizing feeling. This is something which fulfills both Brie and I. I'm particularly fond of this haiku by Brieanne, which describes this feeling perfectly.

Bodies move together in concert
Only physical entities and breath
One energetic pulse

Through sharing, we've found other interests in common -, particularly music. By a strange coincidence, during one of our first correspondence's, we found out that we have been dedicated fans of the band, *Spiritualized*. This led us to learn that we have a mutual love of experimental rock and electronic music; something we both use to inspire our art and find motivates our creative writing.

Brieanne, a prolific and talented writer; includes several of her haiku and longer poems in this book. She learned from an early age, to use imagination and poetry to document life stories, significant moments and other matters.

In this publication, you will get to know Brieanne, through parallels with the main character, Liv. Brieanne uses a vignette of short stories, photography, poetry, and artwork to express human failings, suffering, and loss. She also uses her creativity to shine a spotlight on current events and human error. Liv literally lives through a myriad of negative events, but through her creative spirit, she learns how to continue living, and ultimately grow. Brie's devotion to writing, yoga, and meditation, guides her through life's experiences; just as it healed Liv through a series of traumatic events.

It has been an absolute privilege to be asked by my dear friend Brieanne, to write the foreword and illustrate two images for Purge-A-Tory. Brie is a remarkable woman who was inspired to create a captivating story and tells it in a non-conventional way. Similar to the way Brie has reformed her life, I aspire that Purge-A-Tory will inspire others to change, and know that change is possible. Finally, I urge you to buy this book and tell your friends about it. I believe this book has the potential to become the next "A Child Called It" - the number one bestseller by Dave Pelzer.

By Rebecca Goldthorpe

Also known as Soaring Skylark on writing applications - a Tai Chi enthusiast and lover of British tea with cake. An artist; photographer and all round creative. A friend, encourager, and motivator. The Skylark Challenge creator on Lettrs.com, a Lettrist; creative writer and a devotee of nature. As English as eating afternoon tea with napkins!

Preface

This collection of vignettes and micro poetry came to fruition after three years of solitude, while raising my son, in a new state, with few friends, and a small support system. During this quiet time spent in reflection, I was able to practice *svadhyaya*, one of the *eight limbs* of *yoga*. I also began writing haiku, blogs, and poetry after my son was born and researching topics such as reincarnation, psilocybin used for therapeutic purposes, and practicing mantra. The inspiration to write derived from events in my own life. My intention behind this book is to help others as well as; the need to write cathartically to heal my own life I've always been one to connect the dots, per say, and put the pieces of the puzzle together. However, with the spare time the universe granted me I was able to put together some content based on my own life experiences.

I've been writing poetry since I was a child but forgot about writing for many years. I acted out in all different ways to cope with the reality or karma card I was dealt. Thus these experiences gave me a foundation and muse for my book. My therapist calls me a creative spirit for creating mechanisms to escape pain throughout my life. That inability to express myself through verbalizing words and comprehend what was going on in my life has created the material for this collection of short stories and poetry. Once I started a daily yoga practice, became sober, and found a therapist, I started jotting down notes, backtracking the events and the emotions that I felt.

Early on, while writing this book, my toddler finagled a Costco size of pomegranate juice. He brought the juice into my bedroom and started to jump on my bed and the entire bottle spilled; seeping through 6 layers of bedding. I immediately thought of the *koshas* and how there are 6 layers to our bodies. Throughout my lifetime, I have pierced through the koshas using various methods: Hatha yoga, Ayurvedic Cleanses and mind altering substances and underneath all of us, discovered we share an *Anandamaya kosha*. In yoga, it is called the *Anandamaya Kosha*. Ananda means bliss, and it is the closest layer to your deepest self, the atman. In Sanskrit, *"Atman,* is the self or soul."[1]

Throughout careful review of my life experiences and while writing this book, I have noted parallels to Louise Hay's "You can Heal Your Life" Although there are some intertwining themes, I have applied what I've learned from her book to a fictional character's life. Additionally, I also read my son the book, *The Very Hungry Catterpillar,* which is analogous to my life. I consumed each stage of my life, which ultimately led to a life changing transformation at the age of 28, and a purgation stage.

This publication is not about almost hitting skid row on drugs, and becoming miraculously cured by the healing arts. It is about the in between steps, the long arduous journey, and the investigative mind. The main influences in my personal path are *Ram Dass, Elyse Leeds Acanda*, who introduced me to all facets of yoga, and *Pattabhi Jois* and several of his Ashtanga students who have taught me the eight limbed path. According to the *Yoga Sutras*[2], there are three types of karmas, *prarabda karma, agami karma*, and *sanjita karma*. In a commentary on The Yoga Sutras of Patanjali by Swami Satchinanda, Prarabda karma is described as those karmas being expressed through birth. Agami karma is new karma that we create during this birth, and those waiting in the karmasaya to be fulfilled in future births are sanjita karma. We are born with *samskaras*, patterns etched in our being. The karmas that are acted out during this birth, the *agami karma* are most relevant in this collection of short stories. The new karmas that we create are based on merits, or good deeds, also known as *punya*, or bad deeds. The final karma, *sanjita* is beyond our control and only the cosmic law knows what our future karma

The main character that I created, Liv, finds truth through writing, ingesting psychedelics, music, and finally yoga. Throughout her quest for truth and love, she stumbles over many roadblocks or obstacles, which strengthen her. Each bump in the road is a current event: drug addiction, sexual assault, child abuse, mental illness, police negligence, witnessing a suicide, a mysterious unresolved death of her twin flame, racism, and finally being part of a narcissistic family dynamic. I weave several mediums such as my basic knowledge of yoga and psychology and integrate poetry, micro poetry, haiku, vignettes, and artwork into a tapestry in order to convey the stages of Liv's life.

Acknowledgments

A lineage of Ashtanga Yoga Teachers past and present, Stair Calhoun and Tova Steiner, my current yoga teachers at *Ashtanga Yoga Ann Arbor*: Angela Jamison & Rachel Garcia, artists: Rebecca Goldthorpe, Janessa Rohweller, Lauren Bennett, Carolina Vasquez, Tricia Giannetta, Ginger Blair, Rob Lootens, Melissa (Misa) Goronno, Margaret Shaw Watson, Elyse Leeds Acanda, the *lettrs* application, a registered trademark, *Ku, a creative social network*, Louise Hay and her book, "You can Heal Your Life," the *Hay House*, and *Balboa press*.

Introduction

In this collection of prose, photography, artwork, poetry, haiku and micro poetry, I write about some of the traumas Liv Weld experienced, her story and how she healed herself through purification methods. I incorporate my knowledge of psychology, Eastern philosophy, and creativity to explore a spirit's journey and her "will to live" Liv is a loner in this lifetime. However, she breaks through the karma she was born with, to discover the world from a spiritual, but objective viewpoint.

Prologue

Larva-Duhkham.

Liv doesn't know exactly when it happened, much less why it happened, but one day that bright, blond-haired, athletic boy whom she called her brother didn't walk in the door anymore. Instead, an apathetic, angry pubescent kid she no longer recognized would enter the door. His breath smelled of cigarettes now, specifically Marlboro reds. She was sure black lent had already coated his lungs. His clothes were grungy and his hair didn't separate, thin and greasy, weighed down and sticky. He was a mirror image of the late Kurt Cobain with a hoarse voice and the physique of a waif to match the musician's appearance. Reid was just another deadbeat Generation Xer in most people's eyes. His eyes had shrunk. They always seemed to be half-closed, like it was too much of a burden to look at reality as a whole. They used to be wide, bright, and gleaming brown. His greasy hair blocked part of the view as well. Liv would say, "Hello" when she had a chance. She even felt like instigating a good fight one afternoon. However, Reid did not bother defending himself. His music consisted purely of Nirvana. What did *Nirvana* mean anyway? The vibrations of *territorial pissings* ruled the territory of the Weld's house. The only sound emanating from his room was the blaring of his guitar and his crackling voice singing lyrics. There was a certain angst and helplessness in his voice, that Liv knew he never felt. The room right next to hers held so much emotion unlike any that Liv had ever experienced.

Liv had just transferred high schools. Her parent's sent her to parochial school for eight and ninth grade, but Liv felt ostracized. She despised cliques of any kind. She was taller than all the girls, wore doc martins and her skills at soccer and basketball declined. She was categorized as "not popular" and only had one friend, Kel at a public school closer to her residence. Liv begged and pleaded for her parent's to let her go to public school. She hated having an odd name, Lively Sasha, and being overly tall, in a world of petite blondes. She was excited to start public school with Kel, but Reid's disposition haunted her. At nighttime, Liv heard a soft, yet uncontrollable sob beyond the whisper of the radio which put him to sleep. In the morning, his pale, thin body would unexpectedly arise from his bed. At meals, he'd sit there unconcerned and apathetic, not even so much as looking at his food. At other rare times, Reid would have contact with his friends, but only to rehearse songs, not for social intent. His solemn stern expression never seemed to change. He was numb, regardless of how positive or negative the world around him was. Everything seemed to bounce off the outer surface of his body, never reaching his heart, his inner sheaths.

One day Liv walked into a fog of marijuana and cigarettes. She followed the trail, the passageway led her to find an open window in Reid's room. She entered Reid's room reluctantly and tiptoed out onto the roof to find him, looking down from the highest peak of the roof. Liv didn't want to be abrupt and frighten him so that he wouldn't fall. Instead, Liv softly said, "Reid," and he gradually turned towards her and said, "hey," his eyelids pink, his face pale. As if Liv was just anybody, Reid openly indulged in another fresh joint. He inhaled the joint with more purpose than he had for anything else in life.

It was an October day, but there was still a breeze in the air, yet the sun still shined brightly. On the roof standpoint, Liv felt she had a better view of the world than anyone else. It was if Liv was just a speck of the boundless, endless atmosphere. Liv felt as if the sky was her shelter, encircling her from every perspective, warming her with mother nature's beauty. For a brief moment, mesmerized by the scenery, Liv forgot Reid's presence until the pungent essence of marijuana struck her again. Reid seemed to be content in his own world. Liv attempted to interrupt his peace, unsure of how he'd react. Surprisingly, he seemed amused by her genuine interest in his life as she asked him question after question, without interrogating. Liv never criticized his actions, yet inquired about why he performed them and what his motives were. She was the only person that saw him as a lost, hurt, confused person and able to empathize with him.

The days grew colder and bitter as Reid had and winter finally arrived. One night after everyone was fast asleep, Liv heard a tapping at her frosted covered window.

Initially, the frost covered seal hindered her view, but when she squinted she could make out the cigarette light which led her to see Reid's stoned eyes. Liv didn't need to ask, she just knew he needed to talk so she joined him on the roof. She had never been on top of the roof at such an hour. The sky was clearer than any other night she could recall and the air smelled of chimney smoke, the first indication of winter. Liv felt like one of those stars, a speck in the endless sky. Liv initiated the conversation and sensed something was wrong as they talked. Reid was noticeably more depressed than usual. However, she couldn't pinpoint why so they just talked. Reid said, "Do you ever wonder what life would be like if I had never been born?" In response, Liv said, "Yeah, pretty dull, half-jokingly." However, she knew she would be devastated.

The cold air kept them more alert than ever, and open to the eeriness of the night. Liv looked up at the sky and she blinked once to find her restless eyes looking at a shooting star. It seemed to be only miles away. Bewildered and amazed, a rush of peace streamed through her. She has many wishes as most teenage girls do, but her primary wish was for Reid, to be happy again, as he had been as a child. Liv quickly released her wish and the star vanished taking the energy of the wish with it. Meanwhile, Reid was looking in the opposite direction. Liv was so mesmerized by the magnificence she had just witnessed that she didn't bother to let Reid know what she saw. She was speechless. She also wanted the wish to be a secret; as if the star was only intended for her eyes. During the next few hours, they would talk about school, parents, and about the meaning of life. Reid was a new person come night. No more fights, screaming, and threats towards their parents.

As they continued their conversation, dawn settled in and terminated their stay on the roof. The birds awoke and carried on with their own miniscule conversations. Liv began to realize the beauty not only the beauty of nature but the beauty of Reid himself. Inside the house, they were in a different world consisting of chaos and tension, but on the roof, everything negative evaporated into the air.

By the age of eleven, Reid had been recruited to the Olympic Development Program soccer team. He could play the guitar and save a ball that ricocheted off a random player's crown. He could catch a tune, a ball, sing *Nirvana*'s lyrics all the while amusing the world, his audience at large. He snowboarded, smoked cigarettes, played soccer and sailed boats down at the family lake house. He'd often ask Liv to drive him to the local 7-11 to buy a back of smokes, although she only had a learner's permit. One winter ski trip, Liv brought her best friend forever Kelilyn, aka "Kel" down to West Virginia for a ski trip. Liv got into big trouble for saying something that angered her mother so she was not allowed out that night. Instead, Liv stayed inside and wrote; the only escape to this hell she had been born into. Meanwhile, Kel and Reid played pool, smoked a couple cigs and jammed out to some *Dead* at the arcade. That same year, Kel went down to Old Creek Lake with the Weld's.

Upon returning at the end of labor day weekend, the Weld's (Stella and Pete) fell into a huge debacle with Reid. Reid was not fulfilling their expectations. He wanted to play the guitar and write lyrics, but the Weld's wanted him to be on the ODP soccer team. Their "golden child" had failed them. The narcissist identifies with the golden child and provides privileges as long as he does what she wants.[3] He was not going to be a soccer star. The heat escalated and then all Liv could hear was silence. Had Reid escaped to the roof? Liv had learned how to channel her emotions into words. She had her pen in hand but she felt she should exit her bedroom. Reid and Liv shared a bathroom. The bathroom had a toilet and a shower that was separated from the sink. The door to the bathtub was shut. The light was on, but silence. She entered anyway and found Reid hanging. His feet were off the ground and his throat and neck wrapped in black steel rope. He was stark naked. Truth. She screamed louder than she ever had before and collapsed. She thought he was dead.

Don't be fooled by his seeming pride.
He's never felt love; unhinged; he needs to cry.
Leave him be, for now, he's renovating what's inside

Before My Time…

Language was not a word
And earth was not a concept
We knew not of flesh or of sound, it was all inherent
Omniscient cores of the pupil
No question of religion until evil was committed
I knew it all before
I knew it all before
Formulation
But our minds are not simple
And we speak of two worlds
Through our bodies
We are the creators and masters of eternity
Chemistry is our favorite game
But we must remember love is the same
Cradling, Regenerating, Repeating Sins of our own
Reaping and Suffering from Past Seeds Sown
Battling the atoms we chose
Flashing hallucinations of reality stored in our consciousness
Have you ever really lived?
God Is Real
God Is in these Words
A Door ready to be opened whenever you are ready
I knew it all before
I knew it all before
Formulation

Tap lever lightly
This wheel of life I steer
Til' my aura is clear

Baggage Claim

Egg-Karma bud.

In the darkness, she swam and survived, for nine months; not ready to appear in the natural world. This reticence would stay with her for her entire life. Inside she felt abandoned and malnourished so she swallowed her own meconium, out she came, gasping for air with a mouthful of shit. Instead of being baptized, she bathed in a shitstorm. How could a pure being already have so much shit in her lungs, and mouth, her intestines? She remembers choking on meconium and drowning in it before she emerged from her mother. Separation. They took Liv away immediately because she was yellow and had shit in her lungs and all over her body. Stella never got to hold her right away because of the storm. Whose shit was it to claim, "Hers or her mother's?

Her billirubin levels skyrocketed as a result of swallowing all of the meconium. Her skin yellowed by a malfunctioning liver, jaundice[4] to the highest degree, but she lived. The holistic interpretation of jaundice is internal and external prejudice and unbalanced reason. They named her "Liv," her full name Lively Sasha Weld.

And live she did, she lived a good life for four days in the hospital after lying in rays of artificial sunlight. The light nourished her back to normal. Lively, endowed with a head full of black hair; had a ruddy complexion. She was a hefty baby, 8 pounds, and 8 ounces. Bright brownish, greenish, purplish eyes and pink lips, her mom fell in love with her appearance after that stormy night passed.

Liv's parents weren't in the hospital with her for days while she was being fed by the light, not nourished by her parents. She was born in at Children's Hospital in the heart of Washington, DC: 111 Michigan Ave NW, Washington DC 20010. The breastfeeding approach didn't work. There had been no skin to skin contact during the first five days of Liv's birth. Stella was engorged for days while Liv was kept in the NICU. Stella's friends helped her release the breastmilk by giving her a couple of beers. Oh well, Liv's Mom Estella had a beautiful baby to show off to the world. She gathered all her porcelain, French laced dressed and wrapped Liv into bundles of dainty threads.

Liv was born in September. The exact day was September 5, the full moon was visible at 99% at 5:18 in the morning during a fierce Hurricane, Hurricane David. David traversed through the east coast coming from the south, specifically east coast in September. The winds howled and hurled through the city until September 9 as Liv stayed quiet. She stayed at peace, stoic in nature, meditative; unsure of how to handle this new world. Who were these people staring at her? Parading her around in outfits? She always looked around, absorbing her environment, internalizing everything. Was she the object or the subject? The puruska or prakriti? Was she pure love or a just an adornment?

In November, at a mere 8 weeks, Liv was entered into a beautiful baby contest. All she could do was dilate her purplish eyes and look at these people who were judging her on her appearance. Perhaps her mother, Estella was slightly peeved when Liv only received a 2nd place. Liv absorbed these vibrations immediately. She wasn't beautiful enough. She didn't know how to be pretty. She still thought love was a state of being. Liv slept silently alone, weeping inside a lot and when she was two and a half, her brother, Reid, "Sweet Baby Reid," was born. He was adorable and feisty, lovable and full or life. His hair was white straw blonde and his eyes brown, bright eyed. He was fussy and demanded a lot of attention. At age 2, Liv asked Estella, "Mom, can we make him go away? How do we get rid of him?" Estella reacted vehemently! She said, "Don't ever say something like that! Reid, golden haired and smiley, full of game, was their golden child. He was a projection of Estella, full of life, demanded the center of attention, and ran the show.

Eatin' up Life, Digesting to Transform
Artwork by Rebecca Goldthorpe

As Liv grew, she found herself longer and bigger than the other boys and girls. Physically, she had received her father's genes: a big frame, extremely fine hair, and wide feet. She also developed extremely uncomfortable asthma[5]. Asthma is often an underlying sign that there one feels they don't have the right to exist. Asthmatic children often have "overdeveloped consciences." According to Louise Hay, they internalize feeling guilty for whatever wrong happens in the environment. They feel unworthy, guilty and like they need to be punished. However, she was still pretty enough as a child to meet Stella's standards. As a matter of fact, she was handpicked by Stella to be a flower girl in a local wedding. Flowers always make everything prettier. Liv could have cared less about the frills and fancy curls and trinkets. She embarrassed Stella by dropping all the flowers out of the basket and tossing the rest. She didn't understand what a spectacle she was supposed to be and why it mattered but Stella wasn't happy.

In the meantime, Reid was outshining Liv on every dimension. He was friends with the older kids in the nearby neighborhood and would "moon" them for fun. Everybody loved this kid. He was a whoopy cushion carrying, dare devilish, maniacal cherub. Without proper permission, he managed his way down the waterslide at the pool before Liv had even tried without a parent. This boy was going to set the world on fire. He had already set a small town in Maryland on fire with his precocious disposition. Once he reached for a ball, it was clear this child was going to be an athlete or hold the entire world in his hands.

After Reid's suicide attempt, Stella ran to the scene and gave Liv a valium. This was the first time Liv had ever ingested any substance besides vitamin C and penicillin. She called Kel to tell her what happened and then she was out cold. She didn't remember anything. The next day when Liv arrived at school, she noticed that Kel wasn't speaking to her. Kel was in the guidance counselor's room and it appeared everyone in the school was consoling Kel. Liv was left alone in the dark again didn't know what to say or who to talk to because Kel was really her only friend. She had changed schools because of the snobbery she faced at St. Joseph's, Liv had already lost several best friends and her grandma, one of her best friends, had died less than two years before. Reid and Kel were her closet pals.

Summer and Fall faded away as quickly as the memory as Reid's suicide attempt. Liv lost her best friend Kel but still had time with Reid. As a matter of fact, the two would play music together. Liv didn't know how to play the guitar but she loved to write lyrics and she was starting to "feel" the grunge generation; generation X was her generation, after all, the most apathetic generation to live and be a part of. She bought into it sometimes, even though she was in the top 25% of her class, she didn't smoke or drink, and she hadn't even kissed a boy yet.

Liv worked diligently on her advanced high school curriculum. She was in AP classes for debate, English, and Literature and immersed herself into the world of literary arts and rhetoric. She worked arduously on school assignments, despite feeling snubbed. Now she was on her own in her own world. She dreamt about the drama club guys. Even though she had never talked to them, they were artsy and spiritual like her, she surmised; just dreamy. They stayed in the dream realm throughout her high school career. Liv never kissed a boy and didn't quite understand why people partied for fun, all she wanted to do was connect. Again, it was just her and her pen.

By the age of 16, Liv's waist size had expanded wider than her high grade scores and marks in school. In her mind, high school academics were everything and outweighed looks, parties, or sports. She did not make the Varsity basketball or soccer team her junior year. She continued to eat herself into oblivion as Stella left her to hang out with her cousins just a town away and be babysat by older cousins. As part of practice for debate, Liv's Teacher, Mrs.Nash, wanted her to get used to speaking in front of a crowd. Liv hand-picked a Bob Dylan poem because it resonated with her and she was beginning to resonate with the beatnik philosophy. She tremored and shook over the words, her ears were sweating, her armpits bled sweat, but the words came out and this was the first taste she had of having her own voice, speaking a truth that resonated with her.

"Paradise, sacrifice, mortality, reality
But the magician is quicker and his game
Is much thicker than blood and blacker than ink
And there's no time to think"- Bob Dylan
Copyright © 1978 by Special Rider Music

A release was felt after the delivery of the words. She felt better after saying Bob Dylan's words of wisdom. The perspiration from her ears felt cathartic. Didn't she know she carried sweat glands there?

Liv broke down one night and she and her mother got into a fight over something petty. Liv couldn't stop crying. It was the one thing she knew how to do well besides eating, studying and writing. She needed a shoulder to cry on, to validate her feelings, but Stella was not in the mood to talk. Stella's breath reaked of Chardonnay and cigarettes and she was talking on the phone to someone, probably about her "golden child" brother, Reid. Liv continued to knock on her door, "Mom, please, I just need to talk." "I don't know what I did that was so bad. "Why won't anyone talk to me in real life?." Mom please!." Her cry for help couldn't have been any clearer. Stella finally opened the door, grabbed Liv by the hair and dragged her across the room and continued to beat her head against an antique dresser.

Liv had long stringy hair parted in the middle. It was not sturdy, thick hair so when Stella took all of it, pulled it and knocked her face repeatedly into the furnished wood, it hurt. Liv was in a stupor. She really had nobody to protect her. Abandonment. Her father hadn't been home in weeks. Her first instinct was to call the police. She jumped for the phone. Stella had already removed the phone outlet from the wall and they continued to fight over it. Then Stella threatened to have a neighbor come over and "take care of her." Liv retreated back to her room in hysterics. She was alone, a loner, a nothing. It is important to note that all narcissists abuse physically, but most do. It enables them to vent their rage at your failure to be the solution to their internal havoc and teach you to fear them.[6] She returned to school the next day and worked on a ceramics project. She had just learned how to make coils out of clay and she decided she would make a butterfly represent the layers of life. Immersed in her new hobby, she blacked out the night before. Everyone loved Stella. Nobody would believe her. Liv's mousy brown hair covered up her head, her ears, her bushy eyebrows covering her light brown eyes. These were eyes that many had never seen. There were truth and clarity in her stare that spoke more than words, but nobody ever looked into her eyes to bother to see.

Teenage Angst

The cruelty of indifference
The persuasion of the cool
Smells like Teen Spirit

Hearts aren't always pretty in pink
Can you see the symbol where nobody looks?
Chewed in a lot

Drowned in a sea of thoughts she gasps for air, she breathes
Treading the waves of her mind, will she ever be free?

Thriving in Darkness, spiraling down the black hole of life, why stay here?
Nothing but strife!

A slave to time, droning tone...
Imprisoned by illusion, not living in a world of abundance

Bound by flesh, afflicted
By attachment, caught in a play
Acting out this life

Your venom spews forth
A kind façade covers vengeance
Taste it all, not only the "Sweet"

~Narcissim~
If you benefit from me, I'll benefit from you
What do you care, and what do you mean?
Those eyes of disguise overemphasized
What ever happened to the apostle's creed?
Do you appreciate the things when they are gone?
Appreciate the things she saw?
Now you're on top and I'm in a hole
As a result of your lying soul."

Raw words,
Trendy Pride; Cavalier Youth has lost what's inside
Contrived Barbie Dolls; Authenticity has died.
Fluffy words expand into marshmallow pies.
Artificial sweeteners tempt me;
Organic naked language tastes better on the tongue.

Uninspired, unamused. Feels like atrophy, from head to toe.

Listless lethargic fake smile, holding hurts within lost hope, misanthrope.

Whirlpools of emotions live in the vast sea of my mind, swirling, bubbling, but I'm not succumbing.
Parameters don't confine, the doors never close here, I'm free the space I dwell inside of me

Trapped in an illusory world, she walks blindly into another day, wheels of karma in full play!

16 years to discover
Molded by the measures of conformity
Stabbed by the anguish of adolescence
Close doors to her inner being
Starved emotions cannot be fed
Carry on, despite the qualms you feel
Keep Living, like it was the life you once led.

Diamond eyes….Never open wide to reality, only viewing the world that is surreal, slipping into an escapade, where fractured roses will never die. The remains crumble into the sky. Aspects of the day fit the puzzle revealed in the silent reverie. Pure childhood moments enter the day. Unreleased desires say what they were meant to say. Little thoughts take control. Forgotten sins reconcile. For time cannot limit the fantasy that lies inside of me.

Saccharin Sweet Smile
Conceals a Corroded Core
Feigning Through her life

Wicked Game of Society. It's so simple to play. Throw your soul away. Arrested Consciousness will become incarcerated

Love Artwork by Janessa Rohweller

Pupa Avidya Purple and Green Bruises Overlapped Wounds that once red bled. Pain created her colorful life.

Lucky Giovano's housed Liv when not bunking at her Aunt Sally's the summer of 97.' Her boss was actually named Boss and he had half an arm. Nobody dared mentioned the mafia around Boss. The boss paid Liv well, and willingly paid her under the table as a bar back, even though she wasn't 18 yet.

On the last night before Liv was due to leave for college, she waited on three tables while bussing and hustling the bar. A party of five entered at the last hour. Overwhelmed, by the demands and the accents, Liv caved in to her reticent nature. She froze up and she stuttered and she forgot a couple of their orders. A gentleman at the table plugged in to her shyness and started asking questions to warm her up. He asked about her nail polish and then asked if she'd seen the movie, "Event Horizon," about hell located in outer space. All Liv could think about was *Sheol*[7] but that was on earth. The table of five consisted of three latino and two causasians. Liv muddled through their thick accents and high demands. Who eats tabasco sauce with Italian food anyway? Her soft eyes comforted him and smoothed over cracks of a jaded grimace, a burden was lifted off of Sid in one glance after looking at Liv. She felt love for the first time. He waited for her at the bar, as Liv closed her station and counted her tips. He drank a Heineken beer as boss stared him down and watched the two leave the authentic Italian bistro; twin flames only separated by 7 years. Sid was 7 years her senior, but age was not a number when it came to soul love.

Musings on Love

To touch the eyes of your world, to penetrate iris made of blue, to connect as one view.
They see each other in the crowd, no words were spoken, for the heart speaks aloud.

Mirage of Warm Hues
Your energy field shines bright
A Magical Sight

Love found in one glance
The drop of a dime, beyond
Dimension and time

Our bond is tightly wound
Moving through planes
Of existence forever

They reunited, rekindled not just a romance, but the religion they once shared.

El Fin
The end gives birth to infinite love
Tonight is forever
And only tomorrow holds their vows
Death awakens curiosities
Marks of much resisted sorrow burden ripe flesh.
Their kiss dampens the fire of the universe
And sparks the beginning of their lives.
Together they created god.
Tonight is forever
And only tomorrow holds their vows.
Clouds of reality disintegrate into oneness and obliterate
A world of order.
And
They walk into a night of black in a world where all reflects all and time is space is matter is life.

Your soul resides in the crevice
Of my visceral fascia, stretching you out, see you on the other side

Her reservoir of sonnets floods into his stream of consciousness poetic osmosis

PurgeAtory

Liv's high G.P.A of 3.6, and status in high school as having high marks 101 out of 425 students, making her within the top 25% of the class. The only reason her grades slipped was because of Physics but she loved language and speech and the literary magazine. She aspired to be a writer, but her parents never really cared. They were out of sight, and out of mind and overly preoccupied with their "Golden Child" Reid. They put all their stocks into his life in the hopes that he would grow up as a preppy golf player and he did just that. He had been sent to Paradise Island," an all male facility for troubled teens 6000 miles south of Hawaii, in Western Samoa. Liv thought to herself, "Samoa, really?" How could Reid be sent to such a primitive place? Were there parents sending him to Hell, where he would be beaten and intimidated, or was it really Paradise? Everyone was gone, she had lost three best friends in the span of three years: Kel, Shell, and Liz, her grandmother, Vivian, and now her brother. She wondered if she hadn't walked in on his suicide attempt, if he would be in a more peaceful place? She rode down to Florida with her mother the next day. Stella was wickedly mean and ignored Liv's fairy tale talk about Sid. She was livid that she hadn't come home the night before on time and made a point to ignore her rather than ask about this new beau. Note, this was the first time Liv had broken her curfew. She didn't care about Stella's nasty attitude, as she was in love and that insulates one for a short period of time from any hurt. They arrived at her new dorm on August 31, 1997, the day Princess Diana passed away.

Settled in the crotch of the United States, Florida, Liv, still, 17, was invited to a beach party. Liv was still a virgin. She hadn't blossomed into a flower, as most of her friends had. However, the Wellbutrin had thinned her out, and the baby fat dissolved. She was all woman with only a couple of extra pounds now. To prepare for the beach party, she found a pair of black pants. They had been her father's firefighter pants with a snap button and a zipper. He never seemed to fluctuate in weight. He had always been 180, 6 feet tall so the pants were baggy on Liv but still flaunted her assets. As her weight declined, she consumed more alcohol and smoked Marlboro reds. Her thighs were able to breathe that night in the black pants. She had extra space to move and the alcohol facilitated a greater freedom. She was breathing, comfortably in her tight virginal skin. Her dorm mate, Linda lent her a black tang top with an intricate pattern and a crocheted shawl to complete her outfit. Her dorm mates also taught her how to apply makeup so that her eyes were smoky seductive and so her lips looked kissable. Her eye liner pointed outwardly, expanding her large hazel eyes, looking as if she was taking in all of the worlds, and understanding it from this pure view. Liv was high in love with Sid, glowing in radiance, her hair was pulled back, and her embellished pointed eyes peaked through a new lens. She had found her twin flame. Naivety. She swallowed two shots of Absolut Limon, a Heineken, a glass of merlot and off to the beach bonfire surfer party she went. She had been warned that the Wellbutrin increases the potency of alcohol, but after the first couple shots, she forgot.

When she arrived, she saw her first cousin, Lenny. Of course, Liv thought to herself, "was this a hallucination?" Lenny and Liv were just nine months apart, the closest in age out of 12 grandchildren and had been best friends throughout the summer of 1992. Lenny's mother and Liv's father were closest in age stemming from a family of five. Liv and Lenny talked about anything and everything from near death experiences to how glows sticks were made. They shared more than just DNA and kinship, but a friendship. Their friendship ended in middle school when Lenny became more popular than Liv. She grew to spite him and regret their intimate conversations. Stella had accused Lenny of providing the substances for one of the many of Reid's overdoses. Stella started rumors and slandered people when she could; a gossipmonger ruined an 18 year old's reputation. Maybe this was why Lenny resided in Florida now? However, water was under the bridge now that they were 17 and 18.

Lenny invited Liv and her dorm mates to another house party afterwards. Once Liv arrived, she noticed some older dudes from her high school were there. In high school, these were the untouchable guys that she had swooned over as if they were celebrities. A flock of the "cool kids" was in her presence. While she slaved over AP classes in high school, she secretly dreamed of being at parties with these guys, but her mother Stella had convinced her she wasn't worthy of the opportunity. To keep herself calm, she inhaled a couple more beers. A Costa Rican seemingly gentleman entertained her with some tunes on his guitar. He offered her shots of tantalizing cherry cheesecake and she compliantly agreed. Taking these shots were easy for Liv, as she was already buzzed and the taste of food still excited her. There was instant trust, familiarity, and ecstasy at the moment. Naivety. Her burnout dorm mate, Vickie, stayed with her, blending in with the surfers, and the *Phish* music. She was high on the killer bud and pleasantly calm. She just kind of smiled at everyone. Her permanent happy face hid behind toasty burnt red dread locks. Once in a while, Vickie would speak in her raspy voice to ask for another beer. They stuck together, while Juan, the Costa Rican with the sombrero, catered to their needs and tapped off their drinks.

Near the end of the party, Juan offered to have Vickie and Liv over. Since Liv knew all these "cool cats" from high school, she saw no harm in complying with Juan's seemingly kind gesture. Two hours later she found herself on his front porch, immobile, and limp. She was aware she was being touched but she couldn't move. Complete Paralysis. Five hours later, she awoke buck naked next to a two-hundred and fifty pound monster. She looked at him and he called her by the wrong name. Deflowered. Bright red rose drops dropped down her thighs and oozed down her shins. A masterpiece of art on her flesh; blue, green and yellow bruises collaged together on the inside of her tender thighs. Liv was numb. She felt light from the rophenal, but her dignity was stripped away. "Oh no!" she thought, What about Sid?" She searched for her clothes to cover up her voluptuous figure. Innocence lost, love lost, her dignity stolen by a beast she trusted.

PurgeAtory

Before she could escape, she heard the front door lock. Vickie was asked to leave so Liv could be forced into coitus against her will. It was just last week, that Liv had experienced true love, the love she used to write about, the love she fantasized about before she had ever kissed a boy, the muse that inspired her poetry before she could actually feel it. Sid had intentionally not stolen her virginity because he was aware of the Statuatory rape law and because he truly loved her. Sid had been her first taste, her first kiss, her first everything. This heathen stole her away. Her submissive nature and low self-esteem allowed it. After all, it was Stella who had beaten the living daylights out of her last year, called her as "big as a house" and ugly.

Liv tried to black out the second round out, but she wasn't blacked out on the Rophenal any longer. She was still feeling woozy. She closed her eyes and tried to go to those imaginary fairy tale places where love really did exist. He penetrated her, perforating her hymen even more. He pierced the deepest part of her vaginal wall, poisoning her flesh with lust and greedy karma. Ouch! She couldn't talk. She couldn't scream. Would Vickie wait for her? Juan had locked her out. Her hymen was not hers anymore. It had been pinched, punctured and poisoned. He had figuratively and literally torn her, broken her, and violated her boundaries. She had intentionally saved herself for someone like Sid, and now the dream was all gone. She had committed the original sin, and just like Adam and Eve, she didn't intend to break her spiritual bond with Sid.

She wrote down some notes to herself:

Her secret ran away last night
Couldn't handle unfaithfulness
No eyes cried, moistness stayed inside
Emotions could not be felt forevermore.
The punishment for a life she tore.
She realized true pain, came in not feeling at all.
One moment, it raced back to the heart in which it dwells.
Soothed the cracks of a grimace of pain.
Truth was needed to sustain

Juan let Liv go after he was fully satiated. Vickie, a true friend waited for her in the complex's parking lot. She was from Florida, and one year older than Liv so she was permitted to bring a car on campus. Vickie offered her a hit of killer bud (KB) and Liv catapulted into a different reality, far away from this mundane matter. She could never tell her parents. She hadn't had a relationship with her father for years now. This batch was laced with PCP and made her more paranoid that people were gossiping about her than usual. Since Stella had spent years gossiping about Liv to Pete and her friends, Liv still lived with a negative ego complex. Everything revolved around her, but it was negative. Her father was busy traveling around the country setting up fire fighter combat challenges. Liv had nobody but this stoned girl Vickie so she dived into the underworld of narcotic escapism wholeheartedly.

She wrote in her journal:

You pricked my heart, deflated it a little, your needle, ingrained, still beating, though, only a scar left now.

On Monday, Liv asked to speak with a guidance counselor about the sexual assault. The counselor assured her these incidents were common. She advised Liv to be careful about how much she drank. Ashamed and embarrassed, she collected all her long black skirts and started wearing exotic eyeliner, kind of like her roommates taught her but with a little spiral at the end of the eyelid. She was a ghost of herself, a made up version of her high school self. Her mother never validated her good grades. She tried to get her parent's attention but nothing ever worked, maybe this would?

soul stealers glare behind the fabric of fall,
paranoia creeps in as ghouls look for prey: haunt hearts
hardened in a shell; as summer of love wraps up

Adult-Klesha, Chrysalis, Cocoon

In early September, Liv's 18th birthday was approaching. She still had bruises on her inner thighs and it hurt to walk. She found a satin skirt with a flower pattern to cover her long body. That skirt stayed on her for several days. The soft material soothed her, not abrasive, or obstructive. She learned to put the memory away, archived it the dark matter of her brain. There were other memories that lived there too, but she had forgotten about them: the image of Reid hanging, the friendship's she had lost in high school: Kel, Lenny, and Shell, the time she saw her grandmother die in person, the time her parent's used a firefighter belt to spank her, the time Stella assaulted her, the time she accidently ate magical brownies and lost her bearings. She had learned to cope with all this through writing, working hard in school, and shoving food down her throat. On her 18th birthday, Liv got her eyebrow pierced, the thinnest gage they had so she didn't morph into a hardcover gothic chick overnight. The needle that pierced her gave her an adrenaline rush. It was nothing like the obtrusive man who violated her entire body. That encounter was more like a nail jamming through her young flesh. Her dorm mates gathered some coins to buy her a moon pie out of the hall vending machine and lit a candle for her. They all smoked a cigarette together and ate the goodies. Liv was still numb from the Rophenol. Her parents didn't call but they sent a care package: some snacks and a letter. At least, they acknowledged Liv had turned 18 and she was out of their hair. They were mad at her for meeting this Sid guy who had a striking resemblance to *Judd Nelson* and, a parent's worst stereotypical nightmare if one was to use looks as a measure of judgment.

Sid surprised her with his first call to Florida from Texas, the pit of the country, with a midnight call. Liv honestly didn't know if he ever would call and she didn't recall telling him this was her 18th birthday, but maybe she had? As Liv picked up her green and pink swatch watch telephone, she felt a warmth in her chest, despite this awful deed she had just partaken in. According to the guidance counselor, it was her fault for drinking too much. How would she ever tell Sid what happened? She couldn't hold back. She loved him already. She could already differentiate between love and lust, but it all happened so fast? Why didn't Sid and Liv meet earlier? Why had the universe set this trap up? She felt like she had eaten the forbidden fruit and ruined true love. Liv was raised Catholic so she understood the basic concepts of the bible. Sid was raving mad, he said, "I knew this would happen." Liv repeatedly, said, "I'm sorry, I didn't mean for this to happen." Sid still loved her to pieces, but would never get over the fact that he was not her first encounter.

Liv's heart belonged to Sid. The next day she died her hair black, just like his. He was from Argentina and was born with thick silky black hair, like a Pantene model. Liv, on the other hand, had an auburn coat of shiny stringy hair that only looked soft liked his when curled and combed. She maintained her 3.6 G.P.A. throughout the fall. She studied English, Film and Philosophy and her need to know more curiosity for knowledge was met. She wrote long papers while high on opium on Plato's rhetoric on "Art as an Imitation of reality." The teacher gave her an A plus on that paper, but an F in grammar, that evened out to a solid B. Liv kept moving on with her life until parent's weekend. She also wrote a paper on her hero, Jim Morrison. She wasn't obsessed with his looks, but with his poetry. She read the gnostic gospels for fun at Sid's recommendation. She began to understand this secret knowledge and wondered when she would be initiated into *gnosis*.[8] Sid asked Liv a lot, "How do you know if you really know someone? Liv didn't analyze his statement. She felt she had known Sid for eons. The question was fair enough and would ring through her head for the rest of her life.

Stella and Pete drove 13 hours to see Liv in October, the designated weekend for parent's to visit their "freshman" children. Liv anticipated their arrival and was looking forward to telling them about her relatively high marks in philosophy and English. She was also salivating for some real food, outside of the cafeteria. As soon as they pulled into the campus, they noticed her new "get up" or outfit and Stella and Pete were appalled! She said, "Oh Pete, look at her, she's disgusting." It wasn't in a nurturing, slightly disappointed way. Stella was incensed with the mere sight of Liv and her parents literally abandoned her, just as they had throughout her lifetime. At the time, Liv thought this was what normal parents did as she always withstood them in her childhood. She thought they would find a hotel nearby or just leave for a while, but to her dismay, they turned around and headed back home. Liv chased after their Dodge Minivan as it coasted through the fine graveled, cobblestone, European streets of St. Augustine. Stella began throwing items out of the back of the caravan: clothes, old school papers, journals, blankets. Liv retrieved what she could and walked in a melancholy manner all the way back to the dorm. They weren't coming back. They weren't there when she needed them as a teenager in high school and they weren't here now. She was attuned to their cold presence, but she honestly did not know why they would leave her stranded. After all, she had just turned 18. They drove home indeed; their vehicle ran on vitriol.

emotion is a language it is
language is a motion, it is
words are only symbols to feel

Vickie was back in their dorm room, getting ready to take a drive downtown. Liv kindly asked if she could have a couple hits of some *Killer Bud*. Liv combed through Vickie's CD collection and found "Skeletons from the Closet" and American Beauty." They listened to some Phish and a couple dead songs: "Box of Rain and "Friend of the Devil", and as Liv transgressed, and felt she had become the music, a friend of Vickie's approached the vehicle. He offered them opium and owned some stained glass rad pipe in the shape of an elephant. Clouds of smoke occupied all the space in the vehicle, except for their blissed out faces. They started hugging, not in a sexual way, but in a euphoric, "I love you man way." During Liv's senior year, she started listening to reggae and the Grateful Dead. She also once had an affinity for Pink Floyd, John Lennon, and Jim Morrison at the age of 14. However, she connected with the lighthearted spirit of it all. She had no idea what a "trip" yet was but this opium buzz made her feel like she was floating on each chord of Jerry Garcia's guitar. Aha! She thought! It must be a prerequisite, listening to "The Dead" before you smoke weed! Jeff, Vickie's friend, well actually, it's the other way around, Liv. You're the exception and they all inhaled ecstatic vibrations and elevated themselves up into a cloud way above the car as "Scarlet Begonias" moved them into unison, dancing way up high into magical realms. Liv saw images of elephants carved into the car's interior. She remembers the elephant telling her something and she began to feel better about life. Little did she know this was he first bonafide experience with Ganesh. According to Man, Man, Myth, and Magic, Ganesh is the elephant –headed god that leads to new beginnings and obstacles. Ganesh creates new walls to block the enterprises that do not worship him and clears obstacles for those that worship him.[9]

Two hours later, Liv found herself bobbing her head repeatedly with a gentle, cool smile like all those splendid "Dead Heads." She was aware of her surroundings and realized she should leave Jeff and Vickie alone for a while. She thanked them for the lift and floated back to the

PurgeAtory

dorm, by foot. At first, she found herself in a labyrinth. She heard echoes of the keyboard from the song, "Scarlet Begonias" in sync with her steps. She was a walking keyboard in a maze. She found the steps to the campus at about the same time she was thinking of the actual word: steps. Was she entering the next step into a new chapter of her life?

She was beginning to fall in love with music, then her new friends, life with drugs. The high dwindled away and she found herself alone in her dorm. Sid called. He must have been calling for a long time because there is no way that was the first time he tried to call that night. Is it possible he connected with her energetically? Liv blushed when she heard his voice and started laughing. Of course, he thought she was drunk and had been with another guy. Buzz kill. The high was gone. Oh, wait, no she was tripping now, that damn killer bud was under the opium. One minute she escalated into the happy realms where all was perfect and then Sid's voice reminded her of the original sin she had committed. Is that what he said, anyway? Who was it that told her drugs cloud reality?. Liv didn't care. Only for a minute, did she remember being blatantly rejected by her parent's, Sid's anger and the emotions of dejection, rejection, numbness took her disorientation to a very confusing level? She tried to maintain the high because nobody was there to ignore her, yell at her, or reject her. This was fun and a way not to have to face this cruel reality. She started to climb up the steps of sleep's embrace. Sleep was waving at her with open arms. For a moment, she wallowed in the middle before delving in. She had this crystalline headspace moment that this life was all a dream and laughed herself into the next dream world.

Five hours later, Liv awoke to the vibrations of her green and pink swatch watch. For a minute, she thought, the phone itself, was trying to communicate with her. He said he was on his way to St. Augustine via a Greyhound bus. Liv squealed in excitement. Here was someone that was going out of his way to prove his love for her. She wept tears of joy. She knew he was angry at her, but it was because he loved her; he wanted to protect her. She had never felt this all encompassing love from another human being. She knew this wasn't just about her looks. This guy really loved her. Although her baby fat was dissolving and her curves became more defined, lengthening her legs and highlighting her bosom, she knew he loved her internally. After all, they had spoken for hours about spirituality, aliens, music and her sparkly purple nail polish. She jotted down a note in her journal:

It's not about looks anyways, it's about how well your spirit fits into your body, the spirit body ratio

Paradoxically, Liv had blossomed into a woman after her virginity was taken. She became more sexual. She had never really had a "sexuality" before, per say. Her shoulder length midnight black hair bounced around. She transcended her teenage ego, stretched it out. Her legs grew and they seemed to stretch out much longer than they ever had before. Although she had stretch marks from years of being obese, her waist shrunk and all of a sudden she carried a Betty Page looking vibe. Many thought she was a goth chick, because of her black bangs, rebellious nature, her apparent drug use, long black skirts, but when she opened her mouth, she was the kindest person you'd ever met. She adopted the "goth" mentality occasionally just to have fun anyway.

She had credibility though. She saw the *Cure* play when she was 16. She was lost at the Capital Center in Washington DC during "*LoveSong*" but the music was so moving that she just stopped and watched Robert Smith. She stopped her monkey mind and felt something spark in her at that concert. She had mutated into a different person from the exterior as a way of coping with her environment, but the burden of pain kept getting larger. This was the next chapter. Some people need catalysts to tell them they are going up the stairs to the next place. Liv had something to give the world now. People were noticing her now for exactly what she wasn't: superficial looks, exterior. Luckily, Liv believed she had some kind of divine help to get through this maze. Otherwise, she may have attempted suicide like her brother she knew and loved more than anyone. Something had pushed them both into the mind state to want to die and both had turned to drugs. Nature or Nurture? Good Karma or Bad? They both had similar interior tapestries and they both wanted to be authentically loved.

Spirit/Metamorphosis-Bodhi[10]

Sid arrived at the Sunshine state via Greyhound during Spring Break. He was disheveled, all in black, his silky hair shiny and jet black. She could smell his pheromones immediately. Was that the initial attraction in the beginning? After they had first met. sometimes he'd call Liv, "Lu." Although he was vehemently mad about the sexual assault, he was still madly in love with his little "Lu." She was the only one who understood him. She had spent endless nights on the phone with him talking about *Terence McKenna* and *Aldous Huxley* and alternate realities. As part of the English curriculum, Liv was required to read *The Metamorphosis* and *The Death of a Salesmen* for homework. Was Liv going through her own metamorphosis? Instead, she decided to schlep around in old motels with Sid. They just needed to be with each other. He brought a couple Ziploc bags of Psilocybin with him. On October 31, 1999, Hollow's eve, they went to a movie theater called *PotBelly's* and drank a couple pitchers of *Coors* Light. Sid fell asleep during the remake of Shakespeare's a *Midsummer's night dream* starring Kevin Kline. At the same theatre, the night before, they watched the movie, *Jackie Brown*. Liv learned a little bit about cocaine and marijuana trade by watching *Jackie Brown*, but

PurgeAtory

she was already living the lifestyle of a Quentin Tarantino character. She and Sid had already smoked up in the lush ghettos of Saint Augustine. Liv played the part of the stoned girl, like Bridget Fonda with the drug dealer boyfriend. She learned to be cool. Since she didn't say much anyway, people thought she was just that, a cool chick.

When they arrived back at the hotel, Sid asked her, "Why don't you ever talk?" He said, "People are going to think you're slow if you never say anything." Liv just looked at him. She had a way of expressing herself with her eye movement and facial expressions. A close family friend once asked her if she had thought about acting. She could communicate volumes without saying a word. In her mind, she thought, "Whatever Sid, I know I'm not right, as her parents had told her all her life." She was ashamed to even be alive. When she was sober she even felt unworthy to be with Sid, but she was unabashedly herself. That ego small self was hunched over, cornered by the world. She was invalidated at her attempts for perfection and most of all she felt fat and ugly without an elixir. At this time in her life, she was only able to come alive through substances. Liv felt safe this time. She didn't know that Sid knew what the underlying problem was besides the sexual assault: abuse: mentally, physically, and verbally by her parents. His empathy stretched out a long way, especially since he loved her, as part of himself. He remembered being beaten badly by his father. He was also told what a dummy he was for being dishonorably discharged from the army. He also created an alternate reality to escape the isolation and shame. The doors to the hotel were locked and she thought, "what's was the worst that could happen?" Only the best happened. Sid opened up the Mexican mushrooms and told her to relax, that just maybe these would help facilitate conversation. Liv has her journal in hand as usual and wrote to herself:

Trees are bare, leaves have fallen.
The veil between two worlds, thin.
Time for spirits to come in!

In the background, she heard *Let it Flow* by *Spiritualized*, and then *The End*, by *the Doors*, a song that surely facilitated her trip. Then her focus was towards the bathroom. She remembered her brother hanging, lifeless, holey dead eyes. She was there again. Her whole body froze and she became catatonic, and then she started to cry hysterically. Within two minutes, the tears turned into ecstasy. Sid wasn't angry anymore either. The cigarettes in the room meant nothing. They had no power or influence over her body. All addictive patterns had ceased. He was just sitting there smiling at her watching her transform into her higher self. Liv could not stop laughing as she was much too young to conceptualize or intellectualize what was going on. All she could do was feel it! Feeling was foreign to her. She could feel her hair growing from the bulb, the contraptions behind her eyes modulating. She was in a state of love, a state of being again, and her soul felt absolutely gorgeous. She had pierced through her sheaths to find the beauty of her soul; something she didn't know she had before when in the ego frame of mind.

Being the introspective that she was, she recorded the following into her journal:

Consciousness Flourishes: Soma

Trickling tears of numbness whistling into the chill of her stare;
in a time of indefinite where, everything defines the end.
no answers to relieve curiosities.
Treading in darkness only, perceiving one side.
The fire in our eyes closes into oblivion.
Sleeping in desires into a mutual crypt behind the hollow
Universal shell. Shadows of their past reflect into the future of time and
We all freeze into the desperation of Living, Seeking, God.

Transhumans travel through time
Tread the ground of earth lightly
Traces of them to transform us

A mime in a maze
Lost in an eternal haze
Speaks to god all day

Black holes carry time
Memories archived in space
Event horizon

Longing for her voice a dimension away in agony
Crescent eyes bleeding through the winds of reality
Waiting for life to disintegrate into the dream she lives for.
Time will never cease, and she speaks…

glowing forms
waves of healing uplift subtle bodies;
a hydrogel of light workers swims out of the black hole.
heavenly chords hold them tight; they're floating in space.

Invalidation

Sid's mom called her on October 16, 1999, the day after Sid passed. Liv was so used to feeling numb, but she finally let everything out. He was always going to be there for her. He was the closest person to her. She had already lost her grandmother, then her brother was taken away, then a couple best friends in high school ditched her, and her own parents basically disowned her. Within just two minutes on the telephone, her heart, and soul, her *twinflame*, was plucked out of this realm. She told Stella and Pete the news and they were as indifferent as the tablecloth in the kitchen. She was inconsolable anyway, but words of comfort to a 19 year old would have been a kind gesture. They left her to cry in the garage for the night. She smoked *Marlboro lights* and *Winstons*, and cried so hard, there was no room to ingest substances. Alone and desolate. She couldn't help but remember her suicide attempt almost a year ago. It was just one year ago that they had tripped on *shrooms* and he had taught her to speak up for herself. All she could do was write a little poem to herself: *A day ago, you passed, I can't capture in the flesh, so I'll picture you in my heart. Drifting down the mainstream. Not grasping conformity, he downfalls into the "underground."*

Loving him a dimension away, reality doesn't cloud the way, worlds apart-together at heart.

Selena said he drowned behind the University of Austin in Texas. He had just relocated to Texas about two weeks prior to his death. Selena and Ariana, his sister, said his remains would be cremated in Austin in a sacred ceremony and that his remains would be sent to Argentina to eternally rest with his grandmother. To Liv, these were just words. Sid was her "other" half and soul mate, maybe even a twin flame and nobody knew or cared. She wondered if Sid was secretly suicidal like she was, and if she had ingested the Shrooms he gave her as a divine inspiration to keep living.

Musings on TwinFlame Relationships

polar
After our rendezvous, I shelved you.
Latent love left on a sill. I chose to
love you deeply, and then I heard you were killed.
my love for you unwavering, as I mourn the
the death of you, our union doesn't divide.
traces of you will always be alive

Fiery eyes lit-embers in a fire; heart thumps with ardor, living for you, my soul's desire.
Two souls destined to meet.
How can this love be? A timeless affinity lives on

Your soliloquy echoes from the depth of me, soul telepathy

His earthbound kisses tingle, as they adjoin in rapture

Flammable love doesn't burn, it ignites two souls, one in the same merging twin flames; alchemy

Lost in the abyss of time, souls learn to find each other again; love never ends

Our bodies tied together like ribbons in a bow.
excitations of consciousness cast into the atmosphere.
we are anchored at last; above ceaseless currents.

Remnants of your nectar on my clothes, crave only your pheromones, sense you when I'm alone Fragrance of Love

Iridescent nebula in your eye,
Opens space for my spirit to fly,
Unbounded love

an aura surrounds your physique
aligning my frequency with yours
bonding without speaking-soul connection

flesh forms as particles unite in utero a soul begins life, born solid mass, emitting light.

Who knows if this love will survive? I thrive knowing that you are alive

Adopted your heart
Owner of unalloyed love
Only for summer

your tender kisses kept me full.
love ripened and a bubble blossomed in my womb.
our indigo child was born with a caul.

Empathy
Together the eyes meet,
Two hearts, one beat
You see each other in the crowd,
No words spoken for the mind speaks aloud.
It doesn't matter if your close or near.
For in the mind, you can see each other clear.
Without each other, the mind is not entire
The bond built will triumph dire.
For in my world, it's just you and I.
The rest of the world is just a lie.
Our souls will be one until eternity says goodbye
Two souls destined to be,
An unspoken affinity
How can this love be? Empathy
A love so strong, never to be broken
A love so unique, but unspoken.

He sprouted from seeds of love
Entered the world in awe
My baby boy emanates joy

a tryst uncovered; although her lover has not been discovered.
she revels while sipping hazelnut coffee.
regardless, he'll still be by her side every night

That look of electric vehemence
Populates my atoms, charging into my skin;
Explosive without touching

Hearts on Display
Language of the soul speaks
Volumes to be said.

Colorful Life

Trudging through QuickSand, Livin' in a
Black and White World as a Caterpillar
Artwork by Rebecca Goldthorpe

In November of 1999, after all, the leaves had fallen and frost settled into the ground, Liv's parents hosted Thanksgiving. She intuitively knew not to bring her new African-American beau, Corbin. They were supposed to meet their friend in DC that night. She laughed and engorged in the perfectly prepared food. Corbin rolled up in his Nissan at around 7 pm. She grabbed her *Espirit* purse and smokes as she said goodbye to everyone who attended. Needless to say, they were afraid he was going to come into the house. As Liv and Corbin departed she noticed that nobody had asked her about her new boyfriend. She also noticed that nobody had invited him in for a piece of pumpkin pie. Doesn't everyone like pumpkin pie? Off they went into the city, away from segregated communities.

Colorless souls run free
Prejudice and pigment matter
To those that can't see

Racism, smelly opinions, rancid onions don't always go well with dinner

Hard Knocks

If they weren't at a rave, they were parked in a vehicle. A week later, Corbin and Liv found themselves in Liv's vehicle, their safe haven. They were listening to some old school jungle music, absorbing the sounds and vibrations, and naturally becoming affectionate. Liv heard a tapping at the driver's seat window. She rolled down the window and saw a gun pointed at her head. Two husky African American men stripped her naked and threw her down on the ground face first. Luckily, Corbin did not put up a fight and was also robbed of all his belongings including his palm pilot. The giant men took Liv's car and everything she owned off into DC. Both Corbin and Liv had to gather what clothing that was to cover their private parts up. They walked a couple blocks down to a lighted house and called the police. The police arrived without a sense of urgency. They were quick to assume that the carjacking incident happened because of a jealous lover of Liv's. Liv lost her vehicle, her purse, and her dignity that night. She also lost her truth. She was still too reticent to speak up for herself. She went along with the fabrication of the police's projected thoughts. Beverly, Corbin's mom called Liv's mom that night and Stella refused to talk to her about the incident because she was embarrassed to deal with people from a different race and class. The police did nothing to find the assailants. Liv felt what it was like to be African-American that night. She trudged through the quicksand of hell, trying to find her voice and breath. The memory of the gun pointed at her head vivid and real. They were sober that night. Liv wasn't treated any differently than the black men. The carjacking was just another proof of the invalidation to her existence. She walked in a black man's shoes that night, just for being with three. Furthermore, she was blamed as the cause of the incident. There was no going back now. That night, she earned some street credibility and a deep heartfelt empathy for the black culture.

The music became a part of her daily routine and the drugs became a part of her weekend regimen. After the ecstasy, she snorted cocaine, which led to crystal meth. Liv inhaled crystal meth, like she would cocaine and her heart almost have out. Liv's street smarts were still developing and the first time she was offered *glass*, she thought she should take in the same dosages as cocaine. She also took yellow jackets, an over the counter stimulant to keep her up at the party. The meth high was so intense that she felt so incredibly alive, but saw ghosts of men hiding behind cars and she was constantly watching her back. She stayed up for three days straight. The comedown was surely a path to death's dungeon. She felt like her lungs were collapsing, and had more vivid hallucinations of a man walking a dog inside Corbin's computer screen. Her asthma became worse and her heart was pounding. She couldn't even take a deep breath. She was dehydrated, her mouth was dry and it took her days to come back down. As her drug knowledge grew, her drug usage grew. Liv also managed to graduate college with a 3.1 GPA from George Mason University, a well-known college in Virginia with a major in Psychology. The next weekend they would celebrate with Oxycodone and more Crystal Meth.

They inhaled crushed crystals on a mirror. Their wide open hungry nostrils fed on faded fury. Their dealer mentioned that some of his friends said they thought that batch may be laced with heroin. Liv went out out to the deck and smoked a Newport, allowing the fiberglass to cut into her throat, and lungs. Flashes of ghosts warped around the cars in the lot. In the other room, she saw Corbin and the dealer handling a gun. Liv knew she was a smoking gun ready to aim at herself.

She saw the devil himself in the mirror behind her, but she felt so high, the devil didn't phase her. Liv looked perfect, like a so-called model. She had finally reached the peak of her beauty. She was five foot 9 and a half, her skin was cleared, she only weighed 140 pounds, her lips were full and red, her eyes oval shaped and her hair mod and soft. *La Femme Nakita* is what Corbin called her. She could have been a seductive narcissist, but she still didn't play on her looks. She still thought love was a state of being. Her heart was pounding. She was an empty soul. She felt like an empty soul, encased by a mannequin's frame. As high as she was, she felt nothing inside her flesh. She found herself in a paradox? Was this hell? Being high with no access to her soul. Was meth the devil's medicine? She was in one of Corbin's friend's apartments and the mirrors encircled her. All she could she was her physical self-pulsating through the room. She was in the middle of the city. Surely, she would be a fatality by the end of the day. She hadn't had water or sleep in three days, just gatorade.

Coming down on meth is the equivalent of hell on earth-or maybe just *Sheol*. She was just a shadow of the authentic Liv. She wondered if this was what Dante was talking about in the *Inferno?* Liv still didn't know that taking just one klonopin would have fixed her panic mode. She was still learning the best street concoctions, the best ways to stay high. Only later would she understand the hardships and adversity were part of the school of earth curriculum. Sometimes, the tingling sensation in her limbs was so intense, she thought she would crash. Another time, she began to lose sight in one eye. She thought it was permanent and believed this was what she deserved. Her chest was sunken in and her bones protruded out of her large frame. She grinded her teeth so intensely that they had lost their ridges.

Through the cracks :otherworldly light
Pebbles, shamrocks, spat chewed up hearts, destination out of sight
I haven't a clue of where I'm going; not a sense of urgency why
Eternal time space, no mind, my ego dies
Although I'm running on a high and feel like I could fly
I can feel the effects subsiding; vacuumed down into the hole of Sheol
Back to the underground, here "I" dwell. No, it's not hell, just my ego trapped in a shell

Once home, her parents gave her a couple Ambien's and sent her to her brother Reid's room. Reid was now in college. All that was left was some trite frame about success with a picture of a golfer and the B sides Aeroplane *Smashing Pumpkins* cds. Seeing the one sides of the *Smashing Pumpkins* collection comforted her and the Ambien took her to another realm. Two angels held her hands. They walked her down in the old street from her old town in Ofton and asked if her if she was ready to continue. One of the angels, Lauren, had been active in the Catholic church with her back when they were kids. She was small boned and tall, overjoyed and positive. Cory, the masculine angel, was one of her secret spiritual crushes in college. Together, they held her tight and asked if she wanted to keep going. She exclaimed, "Yes!" and woke up in a cold sweat, able to breath again.. Liv jotted down some notes, *"These angels I've met along the way, no matter how hard, I try to stray."*

Incision

Liv slept intermittently over the next day or two. Her parents weren't home when she arose, an empty glass house. Liv had already been to a chiropractor and they told her she pinched a nerve. Liv thought for sure she had overreacted to the pain, especially now that she was on another dose of painkillers and benzos. Her mother and father never seemed to care about her health these days and she had nearly died from amphetatmine overdoses in the past year. The doctors informed her that she had a brain tumor that was the size of a grapefruit behind her left parietal lobe. They ordered her to be removed from this emergency room and shuttled by ambulance to the main neurosurgicalpractice surgeon in Fairfax, VA. The tumor was removed that night. The surgeon informed her that she had probably had this tumor for most of her life. It was called a *pilocytic astrocytoma*, and luckily it was benign. Corbin's family found Liv in the hospital. They waited until the end of the night at 7 pm when it was likely that she would not have visitors. They were light skinned. Corbin's little sister looked just like an ivory *Beyonce*.

According to Louise Hay, tumors are false growths. They grow in the body in order to nurse old hurts and shocks caused by building remorse. They manifest as tumors to protect the hurt. Louise uses the analogy of an oyster taking a tiny grain of sand, and to protect itself, grows a hard shell around it.[11] The tumors are also the result of an incorrect computerized belief system. All Liv could process at the time is that she had been through years of crap and now it had manifested into a bulging culmination of crap, a cystic mass that barricaded her brain. However, had she waited any longer to have the tumor removed, it could have caused permanent damage to her brain. At the time, Liv couldn't process all this. She spent two weeks in the hospital recovering. The nurses cleaned her wound everyday and more hydrocephalus fluid was drained from her head. A ventriculoperitoneal shunt was placed in her head because a large amount of cerebrospinal fluid had still accumulated in her brain's ventricles. She never slept a full night while in the hospital and her parent's dropped by occasionally. Once she was released, she stayed with Stella and Pete. This was the longest Corbin and Liv had been separated. He arrived at the Weld's to support Liv. Liv had not been able to wash her hair two weeks because of the giant incision and the shunt in her head. She looked grimey and grungy, but Corbin's presence spoke volumes. Stella and Pete retreated up to their bedroom without saying a word to Corbin or Liv.

She wrapped herself up in her Mom's *Martha Stewart* bedding and finally fell asleep. She slept deeper than she had in years and dreamt she was walking on the beach with someone close to her. All of a sudden, someone approached her from behind and blew her brains out, the entry point being the same place where her tumor had grown. She thought she was dead when she awoke, but with a sigh of relief, she was happy, knowing that maybe she could get by in this lifetime without a blatant blow to the head. The next day she went to a hair stylist who cut her hair in a cutting edge, stylish pixie. Liv had a 4 inch scar from the brain tumor removal incision. The hair that was once there would never grow back so one side of her hair was thicker than the other. Her hair was already frail and fine, so this scar ran deep. She would be reminded of the tumor for the rest of her life, although it was hidden behind her hair, once it grew out. Some girls may care about having luscious locks, but Liv embraced her punky look. The scar tissue was still visible, but after two weeks of being bandaged up, it needed to breath. However, it looked like a hardcore punk/ ravergirl haircut which is exactly the movement she was in to, counterculture.

On Electronic Music

Riding soundwaves, becoming the beats, tempos parallels my frequency, vibrating bass
Her heart sounds like deep bass, her voice is her song, breath is magic, and life is her dance.
Eclectic world of electronic music

Metronome of the heart, in sync with time
Soul patterns beat to the rhyme
Not monotone, a life sublime

On addiction

Inhaled speed before sunlight;
Elevated above earth; combustible chemicals
Melded into the sunshine, now shoes back on this hearth
Fiery hell; the debris, a snapshot of kenopsia
Of my psyche

Drunk on the sun light
Rays of delight filled to the brim
Love pours out of me

the empty kernel of knowledge
dressed up soul
this earthly bondage
one realm above sheol
a drug that escalated me a little higher
left me in this hole
my body sustains like burning coal
caught in the undertow of addiction
mine drowned soul

I've swerved through divergent paths, knocked down obstacles;
turned knobs to catch a glimpse of the astral plane.
death marker, in between planes, a wild lifescape at rest.

Caught in the undertow of addiction, body sustains like burning coal, the drowned soul.

dopamine shots spiked with the thrill
serotonin pop rocks on the tongue
you make this love real

Shaucha: Comin' Clean
Photography by Brieanne K. Tanner

Once only coiling threads, she emerged ! Black as night, stenciled in blue, exploring life anew.

Comin' Clean

Hypnotic after one glass of sake, regressing back to her past life.
She filled her lungs with poison: ammonia, arsenic; back to addiction.
Poof! Her higher self disappeared.
Into dust.
She painted with what focus she had left. A vaccum, a vortex of valium craving vexed vata energy. A vampire that sucked the life out of her own soul. She felt beautiful in the blue glass dress and felt at one with her environment. For a moment before the blue walls came crashing in until she was nothing but greed(lobha). She stared at herself in the face and said goodbye...
With determination, she stepped away from the blue brand of hynotiq alcohol, sake, and benzos.

PurgeAtory

Liv started spending a lot of her free time at the gym. She had downloaded a myriad of old school techno songs on her ipod. The fresh blood flowing through her veins and endorphins released triggered memories from when she was younger. She remembered that rush of serotonin and dopamine she would get when she played soccer and basketball. She had a slight nostalgia and then when she felt the rhythm of the electronic and drum and bass tracks, she felt nostalgic for her times on the dance floor, in which she didn't dance, but absorbed the music. She was uplifted by the music and realized after all those years of attending parties, the music had a strong impact on her mood, not just the psychoactive drugs.

Liv lifted weights, ran on the elliptical and Stairmaster on the daily. She brought her ipod into this new exclusive gym and burnt away calories and stress. One night she decided to try Vinyasa Yoga. She felt like she was marinating in the hot room and releasing toxins, as the class fluctuated between moving fast and holding postures. She woke up sore the next morning. It felt as if a bus had run over her, but she went to work anyway. She had also enrolled in a coed soccer team, the Cherry Blossom 10 miler in Washington, DC, and liked to explore the outdoors. She heeded the call of yoga, though. She started the Friday night *Ashtanga* classes and begin to feel open and calm. Some guy friends would call her to go out clubbing and she would kindly decline. She saved all of her energy for Saturday's *Iyengar* yoga class.

On Sobriety

not a swig of alcohol or puff of smoke for a year
sobriety doesn't need an elixir

This earth, comprised of cliques and clones where dormant drones
roam, but without love, we are here alone.
The bite of gossip gnaws on those not there
Numbing tonics rule this social class, but where is the class? Tic
Toc, Tic Toc

stuck between a memory & her fear; frozen; immobile, the only relief
into the present moment: a single tear

The Path to Complete Sobriety; the path
of yoga, the path of healing
Photo by Brieanne K. Tanner

Yoke

Liv's yoga teacher from the gym, Denise, informed her about a local yoga workshop in *Charlottesville* at *Ashtanga Charlottesville*, VA. Liv had ample amounts of time and a throbbing thirst for this yoga called *Ashtanga*. She had to drive about an hour and a half to get to the barn. Unfortunately, she recorded the wrong address down and Mapquest took her into the city of *Charlottesville*, rather than the country. There was a full moon that night. It was the night of *Guru Purnima*. The moon illuminated her path to the *Shala* barn. She humiliated herself when she had to wake the guru up at 12 am to open the door to the barn. Every *Ashtangi* knows that a full night's sleep is required to take practice the next day. This wasn't her first rookie mistake, but he graciously let her in and welcomed her. She made every *Ashtangi* mistake there was to make, but they still accepted to her. There was one guru that looked just like *Iggy Pop*. He was authentically friendly too, not a mean punk. This new *Ashtanga* community seemed a lot like the rebellious community she was involved in as a teen, only she wasn't taking drugs, she was taking practice; thriving in her individuality. She was a new realm now, where it seemed everyone had a creative side, a yoga practice, and an intention to love.

She had an area reserved for her to sleep in at the top of the barn. That night, Liv only slept 5 hours. She heard all kinds of chaos in nature: screams, howls, an owl hooing, and tree frogs. A rooster woke her up and a blood spot stunned her. She had gone off the birth control pill eight months ago. She had decided to be celibate. She bled the next morning before practice. The moon energy filled her soul with creative energy and her insides with blood. She felt it was the night of the blood moon, her personal reflection. She shed something else that night; something shifted energetically besides the shedding of her uterus. Something more grandiose was transmuted to Liv through the moon and the guru. The guru directly transmitted knowledge just from his presence. He had a thick accent, but she understood what he meant and the light behind his words. His light was as bright as the moon. Is this why the moon in July was called the Guru Moon?. Liv felt horrible for waking this powerful man, so she didn't dare correct him. She learned a long time ago in her urban drug using career, that you respect the man who is in charge, the one that makes you feel good. Even though the guru was not dealing drugs, he was dealing energy and making Liv feel right at home, in a safe *Ashtanga* haven. She saw the guru the next summer, too, the day after the main guru of *Ashtanga* died. She tied these auspicious events together into the universe directing her on this path.

A year later, Liv found herself at a *Mysore*-style workshop. She still didn't quite understand devotion and

PurgeAtory

lineage until she partook in her first week of mysore-style yoga practice with another authorized guru. She had adopted a more organic lifestyle, not necessarily *crunchy*, but she was a full-fledged vegetarian now, and full time-practitioner of all the yogas.

Once she practiced daily for a week, she wondered why nobody had told her about this system? She would have been practicing a long time ago had she known. She remembered being an athlete in high school, that rush, that high, but now she was filling her soul every morning. This was the beginning of her *sadhana* practice. She began to aerate her nicotine and fiberglass infiltrated coated lungs with pure air. The congestion from internal and external stimuli disappeared when she combined the basic principles of *hatha* yoga. She felt her blood boiling and purifying years and years of sludge. The knots in her upper back began to uncoil and she felt the *prana* passing through her *nadis*. She explored the world of *prana* and knew this was a different breath and energy than the empty inhalations and exhalations and sweat she felt while running. She quickly realized she hadn't been breathing correctly her entire life, probably since birth? First of all, she was born with crap in her lungs. Furthermore, her asthma was severe as a child, her drug induced panic attacks from coming down from crystal meth were wickedly painful. She remembered having to gasp for air as it felt like her organs were shutting down. Asthmatic children never grow out of their disease. Although they may not need an inhaler anymore, a trigger may happen later in life, but what really is happening is they are responding to certain circumstances they remember from their childhood.[12] Furthermore, she suffered from PTSD from events that literally paralyzed her emotional body. Therefore, sometimes she would forget to breathe. Through constant practice or *sadhana*, she began to dissolve the accumulated traumas in her body. Although a memory often accompanied the release, her state of yoga and ability to detach allowed her to let go.

Dharma

Every morning, she woke up breathing incorrectly, in a state of panic, anxiety, and depression and every morning she found her way to the mat. She began to breathe into the present moment and then she started having flashbacks, Whoa! She quickly realized meditation induced flashbacks were more intense than psilocybin or lsd. She wasn't sure if she had the kundalini rising experience or just a couple really strong yoga practices, but she was looking at life from a different angle. It was if her whole life was archived in her body and she was coming to terms with it. Liv thought, doesn't this happen at the end of life? Isn't this what happens after death? At that time, she remembered *Pattabhi Jois'* statement about transmigratory existence. Maybe she was being liberated or at the very least shown the doorway to liberation? She had always made the connotation that liberation meant you were free, but she was now beginning to see the process of getting there takes blood, sweat, and tears, not just on a yoga mat, but off of the yoga mat. Crying uncontrollably was the only other way to cure her asthma. Feeling stifled and not able to breathe for oneself is the underlying reason for asthma.[13] One thing she did know is she had found the purpose of life. As an aspirant and seeker, she was on her way to liberation, even it took 200 more lifetimes, and never mastering *Scorpion Handstand* in this lifetime. She jotted down a couple haiku and notes and began to relive the memories her body stored. Throughout the rest of her life, Liv seemed to reside strategically next to an authentic yoga Shala with real gurus. Each one punky, and rebellious infusing their spirit with hers. The gurus manifested in all different forms. Her favorite was a spunky sprite, a small package full of potent power.

Guru Blood Moon,
Artwork by Brieanne K. Tanner

Musings On Yoga and Reincarnation

~Samskaras~
I move through this maze
Day after days
Some days I think I've found the way out,
But I've really just turned one miniscule corner, only to realize it's another phase
So I keep treading through this thick sand looking for other ways.
Accepting there is no way out right now, that you understand my craze.
Maybe I don't need to leave anyway?
Because together we've created this lovely blaze, without being in a haze.
Not in this lifetime, anyways…..

Turning in, tuning in, filtering out the noise and chatter, creating peace within that extends into the consciousness of others.

Navigating through space and time lost in the maze of the cosmos, destination infinite

Shadow of a sphere
Energy marks on our brow
Not then, not when; now

Comraderie with the self
Overjoyed in solitude, isolation
Teaches us REAL love

*Energy of tears evaporates into the universe, what we breath remnants
Of tears; joy and sorrow*

*Nature's whistle blows
Unharnessed energy
All that was static now flows*

*The breath of the god
Makes life circulate, prana stirs the cosmos around*

*Gazing Inside, I can see, the path my soul has chosen to "be."
Clearing out what is not me, I step deep into my own reality.
Walking ahead, a steady line
The objective in place, ego's cries lie to rest.
At a natural pace, breathe free
Through what is true
Stepping outside away from these seeds that made me…
Mind's Eye Directs
Back to the plan, to the root, to Love.*

Born into this world, innocent and pure, ideas and notions of what I should do. What is right? How should I feel created a distorted ego perception of "me." This "me", I hope has broken out of the webs and patterns of ignorance. The insight into why everything happened was "clear" and it all made sense. Action and Reaction. These negative thoughts that cause self-doubt and anxiety are a result of conditioning, not my true, eternal self. I was conditioned to feel like this.
Suddenly, I love everyone. We have all had lived created by someone else's patterns, imprints, and we internalized this as "me", "I", and "you." As painful as it is to wallow in the mind's creations, and

learn lessons, on the contrary, it is just as joyful to be liberated and detached from suffering. Shedding my karmas daily, going deeper and deeper inside to the essence of a lighthearted joy, of forgiving ness, and of infinite love.

Here I am, so clear and so right jumbled pictures of my mind, not of this body, not to bind. Breath of Light, so free, so right. Life unfolds, nature changes but here I am inside. In here, may the truth reside?

Senses pull within, harnessing energy, the inner world, the inner realm buddhame

sticky samsaras circulate
creating this thing called "me."
with practice, i uncurl these
imprints, only love will satiate

when the veil is the thinnest i pray.
dark mornings remind me of the lights in my life.
thrice blessed, i discipline myself to remember this everyday.

Fire burns in dark knight
Death of ego, eternal soul rises
Phoenix destroys illusion

As the ego grows~
Repressing what the soul knows~
All of us regress~

Brieanne K. Tanner

Somber soul sits in silence
Still steeped in mud, beautiful
Bud emerges out of murk

A mind as still as glass
Colorless emotions won't stain my peace at last

Marshmallow clouds drift on…by my periphereal
Stick to nothing on this plane

no boundaries. didn't you see the sign? no wake!
now thoughts of you undulate; muddle my mind
will i ever get a break? a chance to meditate?

Fusing the subtle
With the phenomenal world
Morning Alchemy

Truth be told, not to scold
Angels Guide, until you've died
Believe in you, love can renew

How did I breathe like that?
Escape from mind prisons, Daily yoga practice maintain me.

Ayurveda
Spirit Triumphs all, crack the shell so the ego breaks
The path that liberates
Ghee

A stream of golden paste
Not seasoned to taste
Flushing the toxins, the waste

Egos swarm around
Drop dead like swatted fire flies
Still, spirit lives on

Awake the senses, interpret reality, surely this is a dream
Unconscious slipping into a void, Meditation that space in between
For nothing is as it seems.

Internal gaze, breath with sound
Add subtle movement, the heart will grow, find your flow

Light body awakes
Cracked the shell of ego
Perfect absorption of divine nature

Extinguishing seeds of desire, pure intentions come to fruition, the matrix of manifestation

imbued with vidya
illuminating a path
to end the illusion

Tears trickle drip down
Emotion could now be felt
Cold frozen heart melts

When thoughts dissipate, I'm in a state of being, I love everything, seen & unseen. All is love when you are love. All is Brahman. Extinguish the ego, tame tumultuous tides of the thoughts become nothing, self will arise.

I drew you before birth; I sketched you stone cold, trapped in a lie, so I could liberate you. now come undone as I wait by the sea, lovesick

With a notion we thrive dreidel spins, meaning on each side, consciousness rolls on

It's a godsend, this way our energies blend, close to you We don't have to touch skin Although I must refrain, this feeling I can't explain, the energy in these words contained

The dance of life-not part of this show, yet I dance with you anyway, soul guide ego's pride

In bardo, just a figment of my muse Spirit un interrupted

For the next form:
*Codify document imprint
impressions captured record
samskara for next life memories*

Cosmic Tree of Life
a garland of holy heart strings shrouds
paradise, sheol once under the trunks now is earth
let's keep walking through the homage of the divine

Memories of a colorful life encapsulated in tears. Cleansing the spirit til' it's crystal clear. Drip down into next form. Letting go with Love. Fluidity.

devour nothingness to die
fold in swallow breath
wash it down-rebirth

Consciousness befalls, once night falls and we forget our true nature, love.

Surrender to earth, Spirit not bound by body, Surrender to breath

Your ego will die, clinging causes suffering, let go of "all" of you

Practice evokes wisdom, melding body and breath, shift consciousness daily

Stay on the path of Ashtanga. Stay strong, steadfast, and disregard distractions. Use your intuition and appear light and weightless like a single lead. Don't let the world out there defeat you.

Brieanne K. Tanner

Ashtanga Mysore Musings:

Bodies move together in concert
Only physical entities and breath
One energetic pulse

Bathed in fresh sweat, sanctifying
Spirit in physical prayer, shedding
Egos, Mysore Ashtanga purifies

Cleaning the palate of the soul,
My alveoli are the bristles, the agent breathing in fresh energy
Starting with the body.

Caught in a whirling wheel of chaos, my lives spinning into a windstorm, but still I see an apparition of you, flying through time, I capture the core layer of your subtle sheath, the rest of you evaporates, you're flickering in the wind—steady although my heart is fluttering uplifted into sweet svarga loka[14]—your light body meets my flesh again. my feet are stuck, grounded in the heavy earth, but my soul tasted nirvana. the connection of flames is paradise. moksha in the next life. reaching but not craving, this is my last incarnation. a state of equilibrium, stay balanced stand strong on this turf of time.

AUM=
A wake the senses interpret reality, surely this is a dream...
U nconscious slipping into a void
M editation that space in between
For nothing is as it seems

PurgeAtory

Wearing my hat of dharma
Striving to beat this wheel of karma
Imprints mark; each year a coil
A once dirty life; now made of fresh nourished soil

> Om
> Bhur
>
> infused with mantra
>
> tuning in to tune out noise
>
> mind's eye opens wide
>
> Bhuva
> Swaha

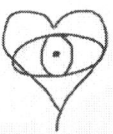

Mantra created on Ku application,
a creative social network

There was no difference between the practice of mantra and the sun saluations she had learned from the *Ashtanga* guru. They were part of the same devotional practice in *Ashtanga* yoga. As a matter of fact, Liv learned to combine the two come from the same school of *Ashtanga* yoga. Liv briefly studied the yoga sutras and mantras in the *Beloved Yoga Teacher Training*. She learned to chant along to the *Gayatri Mantra*, but it wasn't until much later that she learned the first 7 energetic sounds correlated to the 7 planes of existence in Dante's Paradiso. She simultaneously began practicing *Surya Namaskars* and sometimes parts of the primary series every morning. She bought a copy of the *Yoga Mala* and learned that her approach was correct according to the master guru, *Pattabhi Jois*. The sun saluations and the asana practice combined with the Ashtanga invocation were a "prayer not just for the strength of the body, senses and the mind, but for the elimination of diseases, and to promote inner peace and liberation from transmigratory existence."[15] She was finally doing something right and the inner validation was more than enough to get by.

As Liv began to explore the other facet's of yoga, she became entranced with *mantra*. She remembers the first teacher who introduced her to *mantra*. She was the embodiment of all the goddess' she had read about over the years: *Aphrodite*, *Lakshmi*, and *Sarasvati*. She was a live, in living color, a *Devi*. She sung with the angels and held high notes only the heavenly realms understood. She said the definition of yoga was to feel complete, to need nothing. She was beautiful, in harmony with nature, magical and clever. Her heavenly incantations were transmitted to Liv instantanously. The angels echoed through her as she chanted the mantras and explained to us the five mouth positions. According to Anodea Judith, the sounds in chanting may have meanings that we wish to instill in our consciousness.[16] Anodea says some yogis believe that chanting mantras release a "liquid nectar" within the pineal gland which alters consciousness.[17] Her mouth was musical and Liv caught onto the vibration and chanted one two many times to Sarasvati and found her well of creativity as well.

The mantras she learned echoed throughout her life and would always come back to her if she forgot to say them. Afterall, mantras are meant to protect us. She finally accessed her creative spirit again. She was going deeper and deeper into the yoga matrix. Liv became enchanted with her words and the vibration. The teacher asked each student in the class to explain what sanskrit meant to them and Liv said, "Sanskrit is the absorption of breath and sound, a vinyasa for the tongue. The class continued chanting until the birds outside chimed in and the sun came out. The live goddess was Snow White if she could make the birds sing! Liv not only found her voice, but she felt elevated simply by activating certain positions in her mouth. She resonated with one mantra in particiular, bringing in the energy of the deity, Ganesh: *Om Gam Ganapataye Namaha.* This mantra stuck with her for years. Ganesh had always been around before she called on him. Apparently, he was setting up these obstacles for Liv's path to help her grow. Liv bought her first mala and began to feel the music in her soul, and her pen begin to flow. Once again the universe had presented her with another method to heal. The yoga and mantras helped protect her from negative thought patterns and finally, to not feel ashamed of her once abhorrible past. She felt she had already been reincarnated many times in one lifetime, since she was given this golden opportunity to be free, to find the keys to *moksha,* a taste of liberation.

Deep in the lake country, the Weld's shared a cove with six other retirees. Each couple lost their daughter at some point in their lives. Some deaths were accidents and some died of sepsis and poor health, but now the Weld's had lost their eldest daughter. In the yoga sutras of Patanjali, Swami Satchidananda interprets Book one, 1-33 writes that by cultivating attitudes of friendliness toward the happy, and compassion for the sad, delight in virtuous, and indifference toward the wicked. This is how the mind remains calm.[18] Liv had inevitably become indifferent to her family, as they had been indifferent to her most of her life when she was in crisis. Her brother Reid felt the need to call and harass her when Liv didn't comply with the family's picture perfect image. The golden child can do no wrong and the scapegoat is always at fault. The golden child will defend the mother and indirectly continue abuse by finding reasons to blame the scapegoat.[19]

They still live in a giant glass house on Old Creek Lake, and nobody would dare throw stones at them. They realized she was never coming back into their lives, into that false pretty picture they created. They didn't know she saw through it until she finally ended the pattern. According to Lauren Bennett, the only way to break the narcissist/scapegoat family dynamic is by cutting off contact with the abusive parent, because as long as one continues seeking to please them, they will continue to attempt to break you down and make you feel insignificant.[20] They called her one last time to see if there was a chance at a reunion and Liv said, "I'm sorry, I've become disenchanted with you." Liv meandered her way through the shitstorm and came up for air at last. Everyday, she wakes up fighting both of her parent's karmas: her mother's addiction and narcissistic tendencies and her dad's sullen passive aggressive anger. She practices yoga to change her programming.   Liv never stopped loving her parent's. She believed in pure unconditional love and knew they were capable of it, just not in this lifetime. She mandated herself to sever ties with them and love them from a distance, hoping they would see the same light she saw one day. Her addiction, and depression tendencies and desire to make things right put her in a fragile position. She would only break each time she had an encounter with them. She couldn't walk on egg shells any longer and she had learned in the last couple of years that confronting them, was the equivalent of throwing rocks at their beautiful glass house.

She broke the cycle and the samskaras that she was born with so that her offspring would not inherit the burden, Liv began to let go of all that guilt and shame that her ego had carried around for years, that her soul had carried around for centuries, and she moved into the future, breaking through the so called predetermined patterns she fought so hard to uncoil. She worked hard to purge herself of her ego patterns and transcend her ego, and she wondered if purgatory wasn't in the after life, but here now, where we trudge through the quicksand of hell, and on the light days, climb the escalades of heaven. She lost out on being popular, but she gained a new friend, herself. She realized the authentic connections she did have in her life and she nurtured those friendships. The question that Sid once used to ask, "Does anyone really know anyone?" echoes through her mind everyday. Without love involved, we are all just walking dummies brought together by trends, gossip, and sometimes substances. Liv joined Alcoholics Anonymous and the Ashtaga Yoga Shala in Ann Arbor, Michigan. **A** to the sixth power. That's what the universe gave her for her effort to fix things, to make things right and most of all to allow Liv live to tell this story.

Sanskrit Mantra

A garland of beads
Tangibles for leading prayer.
Bound together by a thread

Melting Rigidity, Ending Monotony
Mind Stops. Beautiful Stream of Consiousness flows through

Yoga is my muse
Evoking feelings that must
be set loose, Clear senses.

Meditation and mantras create
A more miraculous, mysterious &
magical Life beyond matter

my breath surfs the waves of my mind until it coasts smoothly on calm tides, I Am fluidity.

slipping into an escapade
killing ego softly
grim reality begins to fade.

I'm just passing through
I'm not really here to stay
Non attachment phase

Unwinding long coils attached to heart strings, beneath the sheath, an open warm heart.

Spoken words elevate our soul's vibration, the chakras are activated with sound; sanskrit, The power of mantra heals

Paradise
Beyond the lens of the sun
Through seven planes I glide
Words are futile here, this
Feeling I can't describe
Only understood deep inside.

OM
Breath and voice combined
Chords to the chakras refined
A chant to rejoice

Caught in a frame of matter-multifaceted beings created as one and the same

On Nature:

Intricate patterns embedded deep within, pure in color. A unique shape; a delicate snowflake.

Snow kissed branched Shadows reflect barren trees the unadorned beauty of winter

Formed by nature pieces from paleo era the natural bridge

Moist droplets hold light, sequins glimmer in the night, first snowflakes of winter fell tonight.

A lime colored moon sets into a plum aura faint sun; a new day

Bleak blank sky snow sticks to land desolate trees barely stand frigid fresh air awakens me

Skittish Squirrels skedaddle up stark trees on snowy land, still, sun is shining, savoring nature

White Soft petals fall, landing on rugged earth, ephemeral beauty before the elements evaporate

New Moon, New Snow, New Mind
Unadulterated dawn, new day
Wishing it was always this way

Earth exhales~Trees Dance
As Creatures Swoon, buds burgeon
Night of the milk moon

Weeping willows waltz with wind
Wistful wishful thoughts wilt whilst woes wane

Effervescent words perk up
Plush purple posies upon silence bed of flowers bids farewell

Rainbow realms above
Reflect light and vibration
Of pure souls below

PurgeAtory

Soaring Skylark, Artwork by Janessa Rohweller

Poems and Haiku:

A prickly orange pear pokes me, prodding me until I'm piqued!
Ouch! Hurts so good!
Sometimes pain is the only way to let the poison out.

I always told the truth, but a part of me still lied, devils charmed,
angels sighed, til' I realized our love had died

Tears drip, forming a puddle of sorrow, shedding pain today, wishing
for a better tomorrow

Band-aids patch a scarred heart letting go, old hurts clear away now
love is within her reach

Sounds of sobs sedate her to sleep
She rises renewed to white soft snow cools her puffy eyes.

Love is rotating
Circulating around us
Force of existence

A punctured picture won't remove the disdain
I'm cleaning out the poison one drop at at time.
Tears hold memories, but you're out of my heart forever without a stain.

Truants of the time
Kiss truth upon his forehead
Angel in the street

Commotion quiets
Aura heightens, matter stills
Birth of a new day

Decay of fall done
Demise of winter; rebirth
Sleeping blossoms awake

Ground to plant our fleet, ether above, sow our seeds with love this home you give so that we may live

Superfluous feelings float by; fluctuations die; a fleeting time of bliss in the sky

Refined Scribbles & meaningful marks, collective consciousness engraved in my heart

Not always distinct from the crowd, angels uplift us with open wings

Accessing layers of herself, surface lies, role in a script, a play, who am I today?

The unabashed naked prose, connecting worlds
With words, we stay close.

Pregnant, Full of Words
Syllable beats in the womb
Born, a new haiku

A picture can't always convey
What I need to say
Being here with you is something I want to pursue

Words flow into you
Create to find catharsis
Reflections of you

A seamstress of thoughts
Sutures keep words together
Her own dress fits best

Lucid soft eyes paint
Pictures that turn into collages
Frame of perception
The canvas of life

Swallowed by my shadow
Living in reflection
Silhouette without me to follow,
I'm just a shadow

Vagabond vixen in her youth
Evolved into a spiritual hitchhiker

Finally at home; a cosmic dancer

A constellation of souls unite
Clustered as one light
Aligning light workers at night

A fallen ego is necessary for growth on earth, we are here to learn, not to be condemned.

I've exhausted all of my tears of joy
Into a well of love
You've quenched my thirst for more knowledge; agape love
And what's this to become?
There is nothing else to "be."
We are all mere parts, filling a finger in a glove.
Costumes, figurines spinning around, fueled by love.
Connected to the source; never to quell.
Eternally united, there's nothing to show or tell.

Epilogue

Liv found creative ways to cope with the emotional, physical, and spiritual pain inflicted on her as a child. Through suffering immensely, she matured into well balanced human being. She had a vivid imagination, she wrote poems and notes to herself and she found solace in countercultures and subcultures. Since she was emotionally and physically abused from a young age, but she found ways to survive, even though internally, her fight or flight or sympathetic nervous system was activated. She was bashful and shy as a result of being a victim, and unable to express to the world the pain she was going through. After many years of ingesting drug use, toxic relationships, and friendships, Liv finally found herself free from this bondage she born into. She realized it took work to liberate herself from these harmful patterns: an asana practice, staying sober and removing herself from her parents.

The cover, by the artist, Janessa Rohweller, symbolizes Liv's awareness of her Metamorphisis. As a caterpillar, she ingested psychedelics, toxic behaviors, and abuse. The suffering and the drugs she took eventually helped her mature, instead of regress. Luckily, she made it through the warzone of emotional combat with just a couple external visible scars, and a multitude of internal scars. Her wings represent her higher self-, and they could not have soared without the help of the healing arts, involution of the self, and divine intervention. The mouth is sewn shut represents the inability to speak for the majority of her life.

Through self-realization and new found sobriety, she learned that it was not normal to have endured what she went through. Since she was overly timid as a youngster, she never brought attention to the gravity of the situations that damaged her self-esteem even further.

Liv becomes entranced by the idea of reincarnation, wondering why she chose her parents. She realizes there are emotional and spiritual deaths, besides physical deaths. She alludes to the idea that through dedicated and spiritual practices and methods, that one can purge themselves of the negative karma they were born with. By practicing yoga, she destructs that sneaky ego and finds her authentic self.

Afterword

Liv had the opportunity to live out her parent's karma or change the pattern. Through yoga, she was able to shed past negative karmas that seemed to stick to her. Although the psychedelics and early drug use expanded Liv's consciousness and enabled her to see life through another lens, she became addicted to the feeling of being high and the drugs turned on her, almost killing her several times.

Are we in fact in Purge-A-Tory already, purging our past patterns of negative karma to reach a new state of consciousness or a new place after life? The material that Liv wrote as a young child was predictive of her future so she did indeed live out the lyrics of her life. From a spiritual perspective, Liv is practicing yoga to unite with her soul. In the book, *Man, Myth, and Magic*, the goal of yoga is defined as the permanent liberation from the bondage of rebirth in another incarnation.[i] With this knowledge, she is motivated to practice more, knowing that her entire blood family (Family of Origin) has the potential to evolve and eventually love each other purely and unconditionally. Liv practiced several types of yoga throughout the string of vignettes and they all have the same goal.

Reid and Liv both tried to commit suicide, ingested copious amount of drugs and alcohol and rebelled against their parents. This was a clear pattern that Liv realized and it is important to note that early parenting can have a major impact on the outcome of a child's adult life. Throughout the story, different religious concepts and spiritual musings are brought up to show that Liv is a truth seeker, a truth teller and open minded. She has was born into a dysfunctional family.

Sid taught her a lot of valuable lessons in the beginning of her caterpillarness. She ingested a diet consisting of the copious amount of drugs and although she was fulfilled under the influence at times, she was seeking another life, happiness, through a drug. Once she started practicing yoga, she activated the same chemicals in her brain and felt complete at last. Yoga was harder work but forced her to face her harsh reality and not escape into a wonderland. Through Liv's creative outlets, such as writing, and listening to music, she was able to find ways to cope with a traumatic reality as a child. Once she fell off the deep end and started using drugs, she was able to understand that she was suffering from PTSD and realize was a scapegoat in an extremely dysfunctional Narcissistic Family Dynamic. She was stuck in the moment of the witnessing the suicide and in shock. Since her parent's never opened up a dialogue about traumatic events, Liv began to believe a lot of the things that happened to her were normal.

Finally, Liv found the roadmap to purification and

literally turned her life around, realizing the after effects of traumas existed in her own body. After ingesting everything negative, she was able to purify her body; thus purifying her spirit. She learned about *asanas*, the *yoga sutras* and, *mantra*, and *ayurveda*, which all uplifted her frequency and helped her find her purpose in life. She realized that love is a state of being, as she had once felt when she was first born after her lungs were cleared out. There is no "happy ending" in this collection of stories, only the message that through purification methods, one's body, soul, and mind can progress in this lifetime.

Illusions wind around a spool
We're all pre strung
But we are here to fine tune
Our instruments
Access our chords
Sewn strings untangle
Unravel again until
Deep wounds sutured
With a shared thread,
Love

Glossary

Anandamaya kosha- Ananda means bliss, and it is the closest layer to your deepest self, the atman

*Asana-*a Yama of the Eight limbs, a physical posture

*Aphrodite-*Greek Goddess of Love

*Ashtanga-*Eight Limbs in the main philosophy of the Yoga Sutras

*Avidya-*ignorance

*Ayurveda-*sister science of yoga, science of life

Bodhi-(citta) spiritual mind stuff, enlightenment of the mind stuff can be received

Buhva Swaha- a mantra

*Dead-*The Grateful Dead, a rock band

*The Doors-*The Doors, a rock band

*Duhkham-*Suffering

Ganesh- is the elephant –headed god that leads to new beginnings and obstacles

*Glass-*Crystal meth

Guru-one who dispels darkness

Hatha Yoga-the way towards realization through rigorous discipline

Karma-action and the result of the action

Klesha-Obstacle

Kosha (Kosa in Sanskrit)-layer of the body

Lakshmi-Hindu goddess, giver of wealth and prosperity

Lobha-greed, one of the six poisons in Sanskrit

Mantra-Sacred sounds or words

Moksha-Liberation

Mysore-Style-a sequence of asanas also called Ashtanga, a city in India

Nadi (s)-nerves or tubes

Nirvana-a punk grunge rock band

Nirvana (Nirvanam) (nakedness)-Liberation[21] in the buddhist teachings, the state of liberation (2)

Om Bhur-a mantra

Om Gam Ganapataye Namaha-a mantra one can chant to invoke Ganesh

Pattabhi Jois-Original guru of Ashtanga yoga

Prakriti-Everything Material

Prana-Vital Force

Punya-Good Deeds

Purusha-Soul

Sadhana-constant practice

Samskaras-the accumulated residue of past thoughts and actions, habits

Sarasvati-Also spelled Saraswati. Hindu goddess, giver of knowledge and learning

Shala-Yoga House

Shaucha-Cleanliness, a niyama(part of the 8 limbed system) in yoga

Sheol- Another underground realm. There is no difference between the small and great. The inhabitants here have a neboulous like existence. The dead here are often referred to as ghosts. The dead here are mere shadows of the people they once were. (7)

Shrooms-Psilocybin, a species of hallucinogenic mushrooms

Soma-vedic ritual drink

Svadhyaya-Self Study[22]

Svarga Loka-One of the subtle planes of existence (heaven) in Hindu Cosmology

Territorial Pissing-song was written and played by the band Nirvana

Twinflame- the other half of one's soul

Yoga Sutra-guide to Spiritual discipline by Patanjali sutra means thread

Bibliography

1. Pacheco, Rebecca. (2015). *Do your om thing (*p.137*)*. New York, NY: Harper Collins Publishers.

2. Integral Yoga: The Yoga Sutras of Patanjali. (1978). [Integral Yoga] [Patanjali, Yogastra] Translation and Commentary by Swami Satchidananda. *The Yoga Sutras of Patanjali.*(p.96).
Buckingham, VA: Integral Yoga Publications.

3. *Characteristics of Narcissistic Mothers.* (nd). Retrieved May 23, 2016. from http://parrishmiller.com/narcissists.html. .

4. Hay, Louise. (1984). *You can heal your life.* (p.171). Santa Monica, CA: Hay House, Inc.

5. Hay, Louise. (1984) *You can heal your life.* (p.154) Santa Monica, CA: Hay House, Inc.

6. *Characteristics of Narcissistic Mothers.* (nd). Retrieved May 23, 2016. from http://parrishmiller.com/narcissists.html.

7. Bronner, Leah. (2011) *Journey to heaven : exploring Jewish views of the Afterlife.* New York: Urim Publications.

8. Pagel. Elaine. *The Gnostic Gospels.* (1979) New York: A Random House, Inc.

9 *Man, Myth and Magic: Beliefs, Rituals, and Symbols of India.* (2015) (p.23) Cavendish Square Publishing, LLC.: Author

10 Ashley-Ferrand, Thomas. (2010). Gate Mantra for Spiritual Development. Mantras: A Beginner's Guide to the Power of Sacred Sound[cd] Sounds True

11 Hay, Louise. (1984) *You can heal your life.* (p.146) Santa Monica, CA: Hay House, Inc.

12 Hay, Louise. (1984) *You can heal your life.* (p.142) Santa Monica, CA: Hay House, Inc.

13 Hay, Louise. (1984) *You can heal your life.* (p.154) Santa Monica, CA: Hay House, Inc.

14 Bhaskarananda, Swami. (2002) *The Essentials of Hinduism.* (p.147) Seattle: Viveka Press.

15 Jois, Sri K. Pattabhi. (2010). *Yoga Mala.* (p.37). New York: North Point Press.

16 Judith, Anodea. (1996) *Eastern Body, Western Mind.* (p.340). Berkeley, CA: Celestial Arts Publishing.

17 Judith, Anodea. (1996) *Eastern Body, Western Mind.* (p.341). Berkeley, CA: Celestial Arts Publishing.

18 Integral Yoga: The Yoga Sutras of Patanjali. (1978). [Integral Yoga] [Patanjali, Yogastra] Translation and Commentary by Swami Satchidananda. *The Yoga Sutras of Patanjali.*(p.54).
Buckingham, VA: Integral Yoga Publications.

19 *Characteristics of Narcissistic Mothers.* (nd). Retrieved May 23, 2016. from http://parrishmiller.com/narcissists.html

20 Bennett, Lauren. (2016) *It's all about Image: the skewed values of narcissistic families.* Retrieved May 26, 2016 from

http://luckyottershaven.com/2014/11/02/its-all-about-image-the-skewed-values-of-narcissistic-families/

21 Hendry, Hamish. *Yoga Dharma*.(2014). (pps.56-59). Glasglow: Glasglow Print & Design Center

22 Iyengar, BKS. (1966). *Light on Yoga*. (p.38) New York: Schocken Books

Made in the USA
Lexington, KY
26 July 2018